Amazon Paperback ISBN: 979-8-9931908-2-2

E-book ISBN: 979-8-9931908-1-5

Author and Indie Bookstore Exclusive ISBN: 979-8-9931908-0-8

Imprint: Independently published

Cover by Ami, @ami_nsfw on X and Patreon

Author and Indie Bookstore Exclusive only: Page 1 Art by Meluica, @Melucia.art on Instagram

Editing by Saxony Gray, Editing by Gray

Proofreading by Norma Gambini, Norma's Nook Proofreading

A FOX FAMILY SPIN-OFF

unwrap ME

SUMMER O'TOOLE

For the good girls who say fuck it and give being bad a shot.

Before YOU BEGIN

Despite featuring some of the same characters, this book is *nothing* like my previous ones. It is eighty percent smut, zero percent conflict. And plot? Don't know her. There are no serial killers to chase or enemies becoming lovers, just a good ol' romp in the (giraffe barn's) hay with a sprinkle of holiday cheer.

Unwrap Me is a *Fox Family Crime Syndicate* spin-off featuring Roman, a side character you meet in *Make Me* and see throughout the series. However, Ren, our leading lady, is a completely new character. You absolutely do not need to have read any Fox Family books in order to follow and enjoy this story. Timeline wise, this book overlaps with the end of *Dare Me* but doesn't contain any spoilers.

And while I wouldn't classify this as a dark romance, you can still find all content warnings at SummerOto ole.com/content. If you have a question that isn't listed, please do not hesitate to reach out to me at hello@sum merotoole.com.

If the characters' exploration of kink together, particularly free use, inspires your own exploration, please educate yourself with nonfiction resources, as this book is in no way meant to serve as a guide. All kink requires informed consent and prior discussion, but it is especially important for free use because of the large power differential and similarities with CNC.

Stay safe, stay responsible, stay sexy

Guide to the FOX FAMILY

+ = married   — = together, but not married . . . yet | = child

 Cash + Harlow (neé Hargrave) Fox
|
Niamh (pronounced Nee-v) Fox

 Finneas "Finn" + Euphemia "Effie" (neé Luciano) Fox

 Roan (pronounced Roh-n) Fox + Regenia "Reggie" Cortez

 Lochlan Fox—Stella Wright

Important People

Roman Ford: Cash's second, head of security for the Fox Family

Alfie: Harlow's security detail and Roman's shadow (read Alfie's story in *Hung*)

Fox-Owned Establishments in June Harbor

The Fox Den (AKA The Den): Irish pub, also serves as the Fox Family's headquarters. Cash and Harlow live in the penthouse of the apartment complex above.

Phantom Nightclub: opera house turned nightclub.

Peaches Gentlemen's Lounge: strip club and former workplace of Beth King (Harlow's best friend who was murdered by the June Harbor Slayer in book 1).

Author's
NOTE

In the process of writing *Unwrap Me*, I worked with several Black sensitivity readers who provided invaluable feedback, and I am grateful for their contributions to Roman's character and his story. With their help, I have tried to portray him as accurately and with as much care as I can. I hope I have succeeded in that task.

My intention was to write Roman in a way that is respectful and authentic, while being conscious of not writing about a struggle that is unique to Black men, as that is not my story to tell.

I also want to recognize my privilege as a white author and the inherent inequities in the book publishing industry, both traditional and independent, that BIPOC authors face on a daily basis. I hope that I can use my platform to make space for Black authors.

If you're looking for more festive reads, and I encourage you to checkout some of these holiday romances by Black authors:

No Strings Attached by Nouha Jullienne

Hometown Rebound by Danielle Sarah

The Season of Secrets by QB Tyler

A Very Mary Christmas by Brittainy Cherry

Mrs. Claus Is A Serial Killer by Fatima Munroe

Christmas Magic at Holly Oaks by Racquel Henry

Whipped to a Peak by Zea Kayleigh Galan

Three Billionaire Series by A.E. Valdez

Knot Their Cup of Tea by A.J. Shirley

Christmas in Spite of You by KC Mills

A Novel Christmas by Charity Shane

Second Chance Christmas by Jahquel J

The Holiday Switch by Tif Marcelo

Spread Joy by Danielle Allen

Christmas on the Thirteenth Floor by Lee Jacquot

Just a Pretty Face by JS Jasper

Keep an eye out for footnotes to pair specific scenes to the songs that I listened to while writing them. I'd recommend playing the suggested song on repeat until the end of the chapter or scene break unless otherwise noted.

You can also find the full playlist on Spotify at SummerOtoole.com/playlists

"LABOUR - the cacophony"— Paris Paloma

"Drip Off"— Austin Giorgio

"Brutal"—Olivia Rodrigo

"Calm Me"—Vin Bogart

"Crazy"—Ben Goldsmith

"Body"—Rosenfeld

"Potential"—BOBI ANDONOV

"Are You Even Real (feat. Givēon)"—Teddy Swims,
GIVĒON

"I Feel Love"—Freya Ridings

"Gimme Love"—Rosenfeld

"Lights On"—H.E.R.

"Venus"—Mackenzy Mackay

Dusk til Dawn, come on get higher, looking like that, blossom

"Dusk Till Dawn (feat. Sia)"—ZAYN, Sia

"Come On Get Higher"—Matt Nathanson

"Looking Like That"—Mackenzy Mackay

"Blossom"—Dermot Kennedy

"S.L.U.T."—Bea Miller

"Starving"—Hailee Steinfeld, Grey, Zedd

"Peach"—Kevin Abstract

"Heaven Written"—Soldana

"wishlist"—Alaina Castillo

"Sexy Little Christmas"—DYLN

"All I Want For Christmas Is You"—Michael Bublé

"Sexual Healing (Space Captain Remix)"—Hot 8 Brass
Band

MEN ARE STUPID ASSHATS

Ren

It's two weeks before Christmas, and I've never felt prouder. As the events director for June Harbor Zoo's Development Office, I've been working on this night since *last* Christmas. It's a combination of our most popular seasonal spectacle—Zoo Lights—and our most successful single-night campaign—the winter gala—and Rockefeller's lighting of the tree.

The way I've been looking forward to and planning this night down to every last detail, one might assume it's my wedding, not that I've had one.

All the guests are gathered at the entrance of the safari walk, a raised bridge platform that winds through the outdoor African animals exhibit. As I move to the front of the group for my welcome address, I spot Dr. George Lewis Guzman, Lewis to his friends, the zoo veterinarian I've been dating for six months. His flaxen hair is brushed back smartly compared to his usual I-woke-up-this-perfect style, and damn, he looks good in a tux

He's talking to a woman I don't recognize, but I don't recognize half the people here. He sees me and winks, the green eyes I've fallen so in love with silently wishing me luck. He knows how important this night is for me, and—my stomach rocks with butterflies—I have a sneaking suspicion that he's going to propose tonight. It would be just *perfect*. The lights are undeniably romantic, and because of the unseasonably warm weather, I don't have to cover up my gorgeous dress with a shawl. I look beautiful, the zoo looks beautiful, so all that's left is a ring!

I know it's quick, but ours has been a whirlwind romance. And lately, anytime I bring up the event, he acts a little dodgy.

God, my nerves are already in overdrive from wanting everything to go perfectly tonight, but add in my somersaulting giddiness over this potential proposal and my palms are like Niagara Falls. I discreetly wipe them on my silk dress before taking the mic from Eliana, one of my colleagues.

I think I black out, operating on autopilot, having practiced this speech dozens of times in my mirror. Before I know it, I'm jubilantly concluding, "So without further ado, let's light up the zoo!"

A rainbow erupts all around us. Flashing lights make it look like yellow monkeys climb across electric strands of holly. The mane of a lion is an intricate design of bulbs and colors, and a zebra made from wire is striped with purple.

It's utterly dazzling.

Even though I've stared at these plans for probably more hours than I've slept over the past few months, seeing it lit up in the dark night still takes my breath away.

It's better than I imagined, and the astonished cheers and applause from the guests is everything I hoped for and more. My heart is so full—*I did this*. My team and I worked so hard on this, and I couldn't be prouder.

I scan the delighted faces of the crowd to share this moment with Lewis.[1]

---

1. Play "LABOUR - the cacophony "— Paris Paloma

And that's when I wonder if all the stress and late nights have finally caught up with me. *Have I snapped? Am I hallucinating?* Because the boyfriend I thought was going to propose is currently locked in a game of tonsil hockey with someone who is certainly *not* me.

Unless my sudden psychotic break includes out-of-body experiences?

"Ren, is everything okay?" Eliana asks when I don't step aside for the guests to begin their holiday light tour as planned. I hear her but don't look at her.

Instead, I'm transfixed, blinking again and again as if the next time I close and open my eyes, the woman making out with my boyfriend will magically disappear.

"*Ren,*" Eliana whispers again more urgently. She must follow my gaze because the next thing out of her mouth is, "*Oh, shit.*" Eliana is one of the few people at work who know about our relationship. It's not a secret per se, but we wanted to keep things professional and discreet, *drama free.*

She swipes the mic from my hand and welcomes the guests to start their stroll while trying to subtly push me out of the way.

I finally tear my gaze away and smile like a prepro-grammed robot at each person who passes, thanking those who congratulate or commend me without actually hearing them over the pounding in my ears.

When Eliana says something, she sounds miles away. "Hey, at least you went out with a bang. I don't know what we are going to do next year without you."

I nod as if on cue. "Yeah—wait, what do you mean?" I finally process her words.

"Oh my god, you didn't know." Eliana looks mortified.

I feel the blood drain out of my face. "Didn't know what?"

"They're eliminating your position in the new year. I'm so sorry. I assumed you knew," she scoffs. "That son of a bitch. It's just like Jeff to not tell you until after the event."

I'm still so stunned from Lewis that I can't react to the bomb she just dropped with anything more than a mumbled *yeah* as I look over the remaining crowd.

I'm still considering the possibility that I'm imagining everything or perhaps this is just a hyperrealistic stress dream. Because surely Lewis is not walking toward me holding hands with his tonsil-hockey teammate while smiling like everything is perfectly. Fucking. Normal.

Surely, that is not actually happening.

But apparently it is because Eliana hisses beside me, "What do you want me to do? I'll kick him in the balls. I will. I swear to God, Ren, I will."

At that moment, Charles—another member of our team—frantically calls for me while standing next to the event's chef.

"Can you go see what he needs?" I ask her, my feet seemingly cemented in place as Lewis draws closer. *Still fucking smiling*.

"I can kick him in the balls first," Eliana offers again.

"It's okay. *I'm* okay, go, go." I shoo her with a forced laugh. She reluctantly leaves, but not before sending Lewis a ball-withering glare.

They look like a Hollywood power couple. He could pass for a young Robert Redford and her Amal Clooney in a stunning black dress. I demand my lungs to expand and contract with a deep, not-at-all calming breath.

"Ren, it looks amazing. You did an incredible job," Lewis praises.

I want to glow at his words. I've always wanted to impress him—he's a smart, successful vet with unique, exceptional skills. There's literally only two or three other people in the *world* that could do the things he does.

This time, the praise doesn't come with a wash of warmth, but with a dump of ice-cold water as I look down at their hands, fingers laced together, and a shiny gold band around his left ring finger.

I think I'm going to be sick . . . . *Is the ground spinning? Is this what an earthquake feels like? Is this an* actual *earthquake?*

"Lewis says you're responsible for this? It's amazing," the beautiful brunette holding his hand says. *Oh god, she sounds so nice and genuine but*—holy fuck, that is a giant rock on her finger!

"Mm, yeah, well, it was a team effort." I don't know how I manage to speak with my throat feeling increasingly parched.

"Well, you must have quite the team." She laughs and extends her hand.

I stare at it like it suddenly sprouted tentacles.

"Oh right, Ren, this is my wife," Lewis adds with a casual chuckle, as if forgetting to introduce me to *his wife* was as small of a blip as forgetting to ask for soy rather than oat milk.

When I stand unmoving, she pulls her hand back with a polite smile, and I quickly add, waving my hands, "Oh, sorry, sweaty palms. Nerves for the big day—well not *the* big day, it's not my wedding." I guffaw awkwardly and continue to vomit words. "Because I'm not married—but you are, he's your husband and you're his wife—his *married* wife that he *married*."

Oblivious to the real reason for my panic, she lets out a friendly laugh, sympathetic to my filterless ramble.

"I totally get it. I can hardly string a sentence together during my work events." Damn it, she's pretty *and* nice. She nudges him playfully. "And apparently, Lewis is suffering from the same affliction and is unable to fully introduce me: I'm Maria."

I think my jaw actually drops. Or maybe that's my heart plummeting to the bottom of my stomach, a pit growing more and more cavernous.

"*M-Maria*? You have the same name as his sister?" I ask, tripping over my words.

"Oh, no, he only has brothers," his wife says, and for the first time all night, Lewis looks like he finally realized the giant pile of shit he's stepped into.

Because I'm certain he's recalling the same moment I am from a month ago: me on my knees, sucking him off under his desk when his phone rings.

"*I have to take this. It's my sister. But don't stop.*" *He knits his fingers tighter in my hair.* "*Hey, Maria,*" *he answers and swallows a groan when he thrusts to the back of my throat, making me gag.*

I feel slightly uncomfortable doing this while he's on the phone with his sister, but I want to please him. If he's fine with it, I should be too.

His thighs flex and his voice gets tight and rough. "It's just a tickle or something in my throat," he explains when he tries to disguise another coarse moan as a cough.

He pulls harder on my hair, pain biting at my scalp, and I feel his cock throb on my tongue. Despite the circumstances, drawing him to the edge makes my pussy slicken, giving him so much pleasure his voice nearly shakes as he hurriedly wraps up. "Alright, see you later—" His face twists in ecstasy, and he comes in my mouth with hot, thick ropes while biting out a final, "Bye, love you."

"Really? No sisters?" My smile feels brittle, and my shock quickly morphs into anger. "I must be thinking of someone else."

"It happens." Lewis waves it off patronizingly, then places his hand on Maria's lower back. "Well, I'm sure you have a million things to do—we won't keep you any longer."

As he ushers them away, Maria adds warmly, "And it really is spectacular. I hope you find time to enjoy your hard work tonight. It was lovely meeting you!"

Ha. *Right.*

Spectacularly devasting, spectacularly fucked up, s p e c t a c u l a r l y what-could-have-been-the-best-night-of-my-life-turned-into-my-worst.

CONSEQUENCES

Roman

Twelve years ago

The apartment's hallways are silent. Not even B12's obnoxious rat of a dog is yapping at the sound of my heavy footsteps. It's too late for anyone to be awake and too early for any commuters or gym rats to be up. It's just me and the blood on my hands.

Blood spilled while accruing three missed calls from Cass.

There's only numbness where guilt should be.

The man deserved it. The job demanded it.

Life is simple when actions have consequences.

I appreciate simple. I respect simple.

I reach our door and before pulling out my keys, I double-check that the not metaphorical blood on my hands has been fully washed off.

Finding none, I clench all the keys but the one I need in my fist to reduce the jingle, wanting to be as quiet as possible. Though used to my middle of the night returns, Cass is still a light sleeper. But as soon as I step inside the apartment, I know something is off.

Instincts long honed, I've drawn the gun from my shoulder holster before ever consciously deciding too.

My mind catches up as I note the soft glow coming from our bedroom. One of the bedside lamps is on. She should be asleep. My steps quiet to near silence as I move toward the ajar door.

Looking back on this moment, I might realize that somewhere deep down, I knew what I was about to find.

The bed is neatly made, just as I left it. Cass hasn't thrown all the pillows but her favorite onto the floor and the comforter isn't twisted around her sleeping form. It's neat and empty. The lamp illuminates a sheet of paper on my bedside table, and I know if I were to check her closet, it would be neat and empty too.

I holster my gun and pick up the piece of paper.

Roman,
I tried. I really did.
But I can't keep coming in second.
I'm sorry,
Cassandra

I'm not surprised or confused because actions have consequences and this simply is the consequence of mine.

TEARDROPS ON MY GIRAFFE

Ren

Present

I am not the kind of person to get wasted and make a scene at a work event over a guy. That is *not* me.

But apparently, I *am* the kind of person who gets wasted at a work event, then—out of fear of making a scene—hides in the giraffe barn crying in a pile of straw over a guy.

I'm learning a lot about myself tonight. Including that I am the *other* woman.

Silly me thinking I was about to get engaged. Of course, Dr. Lewis isn't going to propose, because he's already married to a perfectly pleasant, beautiful woman who probably has no idea what a raging dickwad her husband is.

He came in my mouth at the same time he told her he loved her. Is that psychopathy? Sociopathy? At the very least, it's some sort of -pathy, right?

I sob into a cloth napkin that I swiped off a table on my way out of the gala.

Looking up at the sound of rustling, I find Belinda's face above her stall. Her giant brown eyes peer down at me, unamused, her thick eyelashes flapping as she sleepily opens and closes them.

"I know, I'm pathetic." I sigh, trying not to burst into tears again.

Oblivious to my pain, Belinda does nothing but stare while her long black tongue flicks out and swirls around her muzzle to pick her nose as I blow mine again.

"Are you mocking me?" I query with a sad laugh. She tilts her head at the end of her long, dappled neck, and I huff. "You can't judge me when Bertrand would never treat you like this."

Despite the fact that giraffes don't form long-term mating pairs in the wild, Bertrand doesn't seem to have eyes for anyone else.

Must be nice.

I drunkenly wonder how long I could live in the giraffe habitat. I could hide in piles of hay until I sneak outside with them in the morning. The heating lamps they put in here during the winter make the temperature quite nice. Even though they're not supposed to, kids are always throwing their snacks into the enclosure. Could I live off discarded Teddy Grahams and french fries?

You know, getting fired might not be that bad if it means I never have to see Lewis again, because if I stay in fundraising, I definitely will.

Donors love him. He's handsome, intelligent, and charming as hell, a powerful combination.

I babble out loud to Belinda, "Oh, and don't forget to add married to that list—"

The barn door opens a crack, and I freeze before dropping back like a reclining chair. I must have forgotten to lock it behind me; I only had a key so we could store some extra chairs in here for the gala.

I'm expecting to hear Eliana or Charles call my name, but instead I'm met with hushed laughter and a woman's giggling voice whispering, "And I thought we'd had sex everywhere."

Oh my god.

I poke my head up a little to see a couple stumbling in, his hands wrapped around her waist and hers cupping his face.

"Can't have you getting bored now, can we, *a chuisle?*" the man responds, ending his question with a husky word that doesn't sound like English.

His dark dirty-blond hair is still styled neatly to match his tuxedo, but her auburn hair is mussed, bobby pins sliding out of place and waves ruffled. I realize why when he pushes her against a wall and shoves his hand into the back of her hair for a passionate, hungry kiss.

My heart races as I waffle on what to do. Do I stay quiet and hope they don't notice me? What if I try to slip out and get caught? Do I say something?

What would I even say? *Oh, hey, before you get down to business, I should let you know it isn't only giraffes in here.*

My panic rises as the longer I wait, the weirder it will ultimately be. Will they think I stayed quiet to watch? Every option is equally mortifying.

But when she reaches for his waistband and he slides the straps of her dress down her shoulders, I am propelled into action.

"Uh . . . um . . . Hi?" They don't hear me. I clear my throat, scratchy from crying, and try again. "Hi, hello."

This time, there's no doubt they hear me. She flattens against the wall with a slight gasp, and he immediately angles himself between her and my voice. He doesn't spot me right away, sunken into the straw as I am. I push to my feet and his head swivels toward the movement, hand shooting under his jacket to the back of his waistband.

When he sees I'm the person who spoke, he visibly relaxes and unwinds his hand. I have the crazy thought he was reaching for a gun, because isn't that always how they do it in the movies? But I quickly brush off the notion as my tendency to catastrophize. It's much more likely I'm overdramatizing the situation than that this man brought a gun to a holiday zoo gala . . . right?

"I don't think guests are allowed in here. I, um, would be happy to guide you back to the festivities," I offer, trying to be diplomatic and polite since they probably paid upward of eight grand to be here tonight. Honestly, for that price, they should be able to fuck in any animal exhibit they want.

I almost release a delirious laugh at the thought of these black-tie events turning into an orgy across the whole zoo. I suck it back down and paint a smile on my face that hopefully says *I have a completely valid and professional reason for being here,* not *please ignore the snot, and by the way, I wasn't talking to myself. I was talking to a giraffe.*

"Right, of course," the woman gushes apologetically. "I'm not quite sure how we stumbled in here."

"I know exactly why I came in here," the man says under his breath with a small smirk, probably thinking I can't hear him, and she tries to inconspicuously nudge him in the ribs.

The woman takes the man's hand and pulls them toward the exit, while I go to the stack of extra foldable chairs and grab one, pretending that was the reason I was here all along.

"Enjoy the rest of your night." My professional facade is betrayed by a wobble in my voice. She stops and turns around.

She pauses and really looks at me. God, I can't imagine the mess she sees. I pray my blonde hair hides the hay that is inevitably sticking out and that my waterproof mascara hasn't let me down.

"Are you okay?" she asks genuinely, tilting her head in concern.

I wave my hand dismissively. "Must be allergies. Hay fever, right?" I force a wholly unconvincing laugh. Her brows only furrow more.

"I don't think that's it." She trails off, prompting me to come clean.

It's extremely unprofessional, but hey, I already caught them trying to have sex in the giraffe barn. My self-restraint is at an all-time low, and I blurt out, "I thought my boyfriend was going to propose tonight, but instead I found out he's married."

"God, what an asshole." Harlow, as she introduced herself, tuts and shakes her head once I finish telling them about Dr. Lewis.

"A real piece of shit," Cash, her husband, emphasizes.

"Come by the Fox's Den anytime"—Harlow squeezes my arm, referring to the Irish pub they own—"and we will plot his demise. Drinks are on us," she promises, and I can't help but laugh.

"That sounds great."

"Good, see you there." She smiles, and there's something fearless and powerful about it, like she can't wait to make Dr. Lewis pay and isn't at all concerned about the consequences.

She wasn't serious though . . . was she?

FELT CRAZY, MIGHT REGRET

Ren

A little bit down the foot path, after leaving the barn, the three of us run into a man Cash and Harlow seem to know. He's tall and, despite being several years older than us, clearly well-built under his suit. The dark navy fabric compliments the cool undertones of his deep brown skin. His cheekbones are high and prominent—I bet he's stunning when he smiles. His drop fade only accentuates the meticulously cared for waves at the top of his head, just like his closely cropped salt-and-pepper beard adds definition to his strong jawline.

He's the most handsome man I've ever seen. And not because of the glasses of Champagne. I thought the same thing the first time I saw him at June Bug Café. And the time after that and the time after that.

I go every morning for a vanilla iced latte, and every morning, I secretly wish he'll be there. I felt so guilty because I had a boyfriend. Especially for the way my stomach would fill with butterflies every time my wish came true. He always stood out, no matter how crowded the café was with the morning rush. His height and broad, strong frame are part of it, sure, but it is more the way he commands himself, his quiet confidence, like there isn't a single room where he wouldn't belong.

Harlow waves her hand between the two of us. "Oh, Roman, this is Ren. We just met."

He glances up at the colorful sign with hand-painted giraffes. "In the giraffe barn?"

"Mm-hmm." Harlow smiles.

Roman repeats, "In the giraffe barn?"

Cash clicks his tongue with a shrug. "We got lost."

"Again, in the giraffe barn?"

"That's what she said, man." Cash smirks and sweeps up Harlow's hand. He claps Roman on the back as he walks away with his wife giggling into his shoulder.

"I don't think they actually got lost," I whisper without any genuine attempt to be quiet.

"Yeah. I got that." He nods with a sigh, like he is used to those two pulling stuff like that.

I cock my head to the side. "Hey, do I know you? You look so familiar."[1]

He tucks his hands in his suit pockets and lifts his chin ever so slightly. "Do I?" His voice and face are emotionless, but there's a smirk in his eyes like he knows I'm lying my ass off.

"June Bug!" I say as if it just came to me. "I've seen you there." We've stood in line together, a few people apart, and exchanged a few polite smiles in passing, but I'm not surprised he doesn't recognize me.

"Hmm." He nods. He's not giving me much, but he also doesn't seem eager to get out of this conversation . . . . I can think of several things we could do that don't involve talking.

The uncharacteristically impulsive thought takes me by surprise. I blame Cash and Harlow for putting the idea in my head, and I blame Lewis for making me feel so off-kilter and reckless.

I feel my cheeks grow hot, as if I said it out loud. What I do end up saying out loud is even more of a shock.

---

1. Play "Drip Off"— Austin Giorgio until the end of the next chapter

"It's Roman, right?" He nods with a lifted eyebrow. "Well, Roman, I threw this event, planned the whole thing, the highlight of my career, yada yada." I wave my hand as if that is all irrelevant. "Point is, I've been a good employee and good girlfriend, only to learn my position is being eliminated and my boyfriend is married.

"I've been everyone's good girl, done everything right, and this is what I get," I finish with an out of breath huff, even though I feel like I'm buzzing with energy, only some of which is the Champagne.

Looking like he's fighting a smile, he nods, amusement in his eyes. "Alright . . ."

It's not necessarily a question, but I answer anyway. "If this is what being good gets me, I might as well try being bad for once."

"Is that so?" He tongues his molars and takes a step forward.

Even just a foot closer, his presence feels so big, like he could swallow me whole.

My pulse hammers. He takes another step forward. I nod. "Yeah." My voice feels shrunken by his closeness. I bite my lip as I meet his dark eyes and reach for his belt.

My fingers are light and hesitant as I hook his waistband.

But the hands he grips my hips with in response are anything but light. And the way he yanks me flush to his hard body is anything but hesitant.

He starts walking me back, and I whisper, "One condition." He pauses, a slight flick of his chin telling me to continue. It doesn't matter how handsome he is or how many times I've swooned in a coffee shop. I'm in no place to start a relationship. Finding myself snotty and crying in a giraffe barn really soured the whole idea. "No numbers, no strings, just tonight."

"Done," he replies quickly. His voice sounds deeper, hungrier.

He continues walking us back until we push through the unlocked barn door. One of his hands wraps around my ass, crushing me against his hips and thick erection. The other snakes to the nape of my neck. His eyes zero in on my lips, and my heart flutters, certain he's going to kiss me, and then—

I gasp as he knits his fingers in my hair and tugs my head back. The feel of him against my front and his commandeering grip makes my stomach swoop and fill with desire.

When he speaks, his voice is taut, as if it takes all his control to stop what we were about to do. "I have a condition of my own."

"Anything," I say breathlessly, and I mean it. I think I would truly do anything to stay in this fever dream.

"You can be bad all you want, as long as you're a good girl for me."

I mean to say *done* or *yes*, instead I squeak a desperate, "*Please*."

"Now that's a sweet whimper—should I make you beg or . . ." He keeps my head still while slowly lowering his. "Should I hike up your dress—" His hand on my ass rucks up the fabric. "And see how wet being bad makes you?" The last four words are whispered so close to my lips that I feel his breath.

I feel like I should be shaking. I've never hooked up in public or with a stranger, especially one who talks like *that*. But his firm hold is so steadying, I find myself lifting onto my toes to close the distance.

As soon as our lips touch, his fingers in my hair loosen. In fact, his whole body seems to melt with relief. But only for a second. Everything about his next movements are powerful and sure. He groans as if starving.

He propels us backward across the dirt and hay-strewn wood floor, never breaking our kiss. His tongue delves into my mouth, and his palm cradles my face. Once he shrugs his suit jacket off one arm, he switches hands to fully remove it, as if he refuses to let me go.

I don't know how he does it. I can hardly manage to keep walking at the same time as his heady kisses. I feel like a doll in his hands.

He pulls away and canvases my face with his gaze, shaking his head. "He's a goddamn idiot," he scoffs as if personally offended.

I don't have to process his words because suddenly he lifts me up. As I'm taken by surprise, my breath catches. He sets me right back down, and I realize he's laid his jacket over a bale of hay for me to sit on. The thoughtful gesture makes something bittersweet twist in my chest as I remember the friction burn on my knees from the leather upholstery in Lewis's car. When I mentioned it, suggesting we switch positions, he said, "Oh, but baby, I'm so close."

I shove the memory away and wrap my hands around Roman's neck, pulling him closer. I whimper as he cups my pussy over my dress.

As if he knew my thoughts had wandered elsewhere, he huskily reminds me, "This pussy is mine tonight." Again, it's not a question, but I still respond by nodding fervently. "Do you have any idea how stunningly beautiful you are?"

This takes me by surprise, and I mumble some incoherent mix of yes-no-sometimes-I don't know.

He isn't pleased with that answer.

"I only have one night, but I'm gonna make sure you know by the end of it."

I fear I stare at him blankly, stupefied. He's so . . . *poetic.* And all I say in return is, "I really want to fuck you."

He laughs—a beautiful, husky sound—and I finally get to see what a vision he is when he smiles. He typically looks sophisticated and striking, but when he smiles, the apples of his cheeks become even more round and full and his eyes crinkle, and he looks straight up adorable.

"I intend to, sweet girl." He gives me a playful smirk and takes a step back, working on his belt. "Now spread those thighs."

I do exactly that, and he steps between them. There's something deeply satisfying about his short, straight to the point orders.

Then he's crashing his lips to mine again and pushing my dress up.

Using both hands, I rush to push his pants over his hips and free his cock. With my knees wide, I plant my feet on the bale. He grips his cock and rocks his pelvis forward. I moan needily as his thick head pushes between my lips and—

"Oh my god, condom!" I gasp, yanking myself out of whatever trance I was in. Roman shakes his head and swallows deeply as if doing the same.

He runs his hand over his hair, breathing heavily. "I don't have one."

"I'm on birth control but . . ." I feel awful and look away.

"It's okay," he says immediately and lifts my chin with his finger and thumb. The pad of his thumb dusts across my bottom lip as the corner of his mouth turns up. He meets my eyes with a confident spark in his. "You'll just have to be a good girl and come on my fingers then."

He cradles my jaw and brings our heads together. His other hand snakes between my legs after tucking himself back into his pants. "Now, let's see how wet a good girl gets being bad." His lips flutter against mine as he speaks, just as featherlight as his fingers teasing apart my lips. He hums, satisfied at the slickness waiting for him.

My breath hitches when he grazes my clit. "*Oh.*"

"God, you're so fucking sweet, responding to my every touch so beautifully," he mutters as if to himself, and the praise drips like warm honey through me. He rests his forehead against mine and caresses up and down my slit with two fingers. I moan against his mouth. The sound is like a switch.

He steals my lips with a feverish kiss and his fingers move harder, faster. But he only teases my entrance. I roll my hips, desperate for him to fill me. I whimper with frustration when that makes him pull his fingers back, his touch painfully light.

"Shh, I'll give you what you need. Relax, I promise I'll make you feel good." I can't help but relax into his command. "If I only have one night, I'm not rushing a second of this."

He strokes my clit until every pass makes my pussy clench. I'm teetering on an edge, ready to fall, and it feels so damn good. My body tingles all the way down to my toes. My cheeks and chest are flushed with heat. My breath only comes in moans and gasps. I can hardly focus on anything else, including kissing him back.

I feel him smile against my lips, then he's trailing his mouth up my jaw and down my neck. His free hand hooks one of my legs around his waist.

He whispers in my ear, "You really do have the prettiest whimpers."

My back bows, and I cry out as he finally plunges his fingers inside me. He curls them and my leg shakes. I hook the other one around his waist too, and it feels good to have him to hold on to as he withdraws his curled fingers before sinking them back into my dripping pussy.

"*Oh, fuhh . . .*" My teeth dig into my bottom lip as he starts to really truly fuck me with his fingers. I wrap my arms tight around his neck, clinging to him as I mewl into the crook of it. His scent is rich and masculine, a sophisticated cologne and a hint of sweat. The next time he strokes that blissful spot inside me, I can't help but bite into the corded muscles of his neck. He grunts at the pain, yet it's still a sound of pleasure.

His two fingers continue thrusting in and out as he adds his thumb to circle my clit. White light bursts behind my eyelids, my toes curl, and my abs clench. A wave builds inside me, a tidal wave. Pressure and desire cresting.

He knits his fingers in the back of my hair again, but this time it's loose and soft. He gently lifts my forehead off his shoulder and dusts his lips across the shell of my ear, making chills run down my spine along with all the other wonderfully overwhelming sensations.

"I know you're close. Your pussy is pulsing . . . so . . . *needy* . . . ," he purrs.

"*Mm-hmm . . .*" I whine, feverish.

"You know, it's a good thing we chose this route." His voice is so rough and gravelly, but the way he slowly rolls out his words makes it feel like smooth leather. "Because your cunt is begging to be filled, and I wouldn't be able to resist. You'd walk out of here dripping. And we can't have the good girl walking around leaking my cum."

"*Oh god . . .*" I mewl. I'm on the verge of shattering.

He chuckles softly at my desperate keen. "You can come for me now, sweet girl."

My eyes fly open at a scraping sound, and I look up to see the barn door cracking open. My heart leaps into my throat. Roman doesn't hear it, his back to the door. It's hard to think straight. I'm about to scramble and push him away when Lewis's head pops in.

Suddenly, I'm thinking crystal clear.

I hold my hand up behind Roman's back and flip Lewis the bird, and I hope it's abundantly clear to him, as Roman makes me come apart with just his fingers, that with him, I faked it every single time.

GOOD GIRLS SWALLOW

Roman

This woman has me un-fucking-raveling.[1]

She looks at me with eyes that reveal every thought in her head. She looks at me with eyes that plead for safety and dominance. She looks at me like . . . like no one has ever touched her the way I am.

I never fuck without protection, *never*. If she hadn't brought it up . . . I was so close to saying fuck it.

I would break every fucking rule for her.

Especially when she's coming apart so damn sweetly like she is right now. Blush crawls up her neck and her

---

1. Continue playing "Drip Off"— Austin Giorgio

breath is hitched and ragged, like she can't even focus on breathing when I'm touching her like this.

Her cunt is fluttering around my fingers, but I swear to God, I can feel the pulse of it around my cock.

She chokes out, "*Oh god . . .*"

I can't help but laugh quietly at the shock in her voice. She's so damn precious. "You can come now for me, sweet girl."

Her thick thighs squeeze my waist and her pussy clenches. My dick strains my pants.

I watch her as she comes, trying to capture every second in my memory. The pink crawling up her pale chest and neck. The expressive pinch between her brows on her heart-shaped face. The strangled quality to her moans. And the beautiful, sated smile that softly spreads on her lips as she comes down.

She exhales contentedly, closing her eyes and rolling her head to the side. When she opens them, the contrast of her pink cheeks makes her blue eyes shine. "Wow." She sighs with a small wriggle of her eyebrows.

Wanting to feel their heat, I trail the back of my hand across her cheek. She hums softly as I do, leaning into my touch. "You are quite something, Ren," I mutter.

She takes my hand from her cheek, cradling it between both of hers and kissing my palm. My stomach rocks. Now, I'm the one having trouble breathing.

Keeping hold of my hand, she sways slightly on the bale and gives me a look that is both flirty and guilty.

"What is it?" I ask.

She kisses my palm again before answering. "I feel"—she scrunches her nose—"kinda bad."

My chest pounds with anxiety. I keep it out of my tone. "Why?"

"You know—" She bobs her head like I should know what she's talking about. When I clearly don't, she adds, "That you didn't get anything out of this."

I think I'd be less surprised if she kicked me in the face.

I pull my hand from her grasp so that I can firmly grab her by both hips. "I didn't get anything from this?" I press our bodies together so she can feel *exactly* how much I got out of this. "I could've come just watching you—shit, I've been leaking in my damn pants since the moment we got in here."

She holds back a giggle. "Really?"

"Really."

Her hand slides down my chest to palm the bulge between us. Lust glazes her eyes. Her lips press together as she silently asks me to give her another order.

God, this girl is going to be my ruin.

My blood heats and my chest swells at the trust she's already given me.

Who am I to deny her now?

I take a few steps back, making space between us.

"But if you want to be a really good girl for me, you'll get on your knees and let me paint that pretty tongue." Her eyes light up as she slides off the bales and onto her knees. She reaches for my waistband. I stop her, saying, "Hands in your lap. Tongue out."

My pants are already undone, so once she does as she's told, I take my cock out. It takes every ounce of control to move slowly, to not rush this moment.

"Now stay just like that," I tell her. "You'll take what I give you."

She nods.

"Good girl," I rumble quietly.

I fist my cock, the crown slick with pre-cum. I rub my thumb over it, then spit on the shaft. She flinches slightly, surprised, but keeps her tongue out. As I start stroking up and down, her eyes become hooded and she squeezes her thighs together. *She really is such a good girl.*

My jaw clenches as I look at her glistening tongue and eager gaze. "*Fuck,*" I groan, my dick getting impossibly harder.

My abs and thighs flex. I'm already so fucking close. I let the underside of my tip graze her tongue and sputter, "*Jesusfuckingchrist.*"

My threadbare control makes her smile, as much as she can with her tongue out. If only she knew how much less in control I feel inside.

"*Didn't get anything out of it,*" I scoff, my voice gruff and strained as I struggle to hold back. I only last a few more strokes before I'm cursing and spilling on her tongue.

I struggle to catch my breath, resting my cock on her outstretched tongue. "You've done so well," I murmur, thumbing the corner of her mouth. She moans softly, eyes fluttering. "Now finish the job." I stand up straight and remove my cock. "Swallow, then clean up the mess you made me make."

She does exactly that. Licking me from the base of my shaft up, paying extra attention to the slit at my tip.

The sparkle of pride in her eyes as she does this is a grating twisting in my chest.

No numbers, no strings, and no way this can ever happen again.

STRAIGHT FROM THE MOVIES

Ren

My stomach was in knots all weekend from knowing Monday would come and I'd have to return to work, only to get fired. Now, it's here and the added potential of seeing Lewis has me sitting in my parked car for thirteen minutes and fifteen seconds. The most I can push it before officially being considered late.[1]

I laugh at myself. A lot of good that thirty minutes of being bad did me. I'm already back to my good-girl habits, stressing over being on time. Not to mention the ever-present worry that Lewis may have told others what he saw. I don't regret it for a single second, but

---

1. Play "Brutal"—Olivia Rodrigo until end of chapter

it's not something I want everyone I work with—well, *worked* with to know.

My legs feel heavy as I cross the parking lot to my building. I'm so emotionally exhausted. I spent half the weekend crying and half the weekend in a stupor, trying to convince myself that the giraffe barn with Roman actually happened.

When I see Dr. Lewis waiting outside the entrance, I feel like I could simply collapse, but the rough asphalt is less than appealing. *Where's Belinda and a pile of hay when you need it?*

I used to get a beautiful rush of butterflies when I'd arrive at work to find him waiting for me, just so he could tell me good morning in person. Now, it's all I can do to keep walking, ignoring him the best I can.

Even when he runs up to me and grabs my arm, I don't look at him as I try not to burst into tears and say, "I'm going to be late. Let me go, please." I hate that my voice cracks. I hate that I say please instead of slapping him in the face, which is what I really want to do.

"You haven't returned any of my calls or texts." He sounds genuinely hurt, genuinely *confused*. I think it's that he sounds like the victim that makes me finally snap.

I rip his hand off me. "Because you're *married!*" I whisper-yell, in case someone passes.

He pleads with my full name, "*Serenity—*"

"No." My heart cracks a little more. "No, Lewis, you don't get to explain or apologize or whatever bullshit is about to come out of your mouth. There is nothing I want to hear from you."

I don't give him a chance to respond. I push inside and head straight for the lobby bathrooms. The door swings closed behind me, and I practically run to the first empty stall.

I bury my face in my hands and scream every cuss word and insult I can think of.

I try to lose myself in writing up the post-event report; if it's the last thing I do here, I'm going to do it right. I fixate on every small detail to get it perfect. Before lunch, I'm meeting with my boss, for what I suspect will be the last time, to supposedly go over said report. It doesn't serve as a great distraction when the event only reminds me of what else happened that night.

Finding out my boyfriend is married was pretty devastating. I was—*am*—furious, but what happened after in the barn has been playing on a loop in my head. My cheeks still flush when I think about the way Roman's demeanor changed from cold and unaffected as he told me to get on my knees to barely holding it together when I did. It was almost like he didn't expect me to but was pleased I did.

It could have been an objectively demeaning situation, me on my knees, following the orders of the man about to come on my tongue, telling me I can only have what he chooses to give me. Lord knows I felt demeaned when Lewis did similar. And Lewis said please. But it didn't feel that way with Roman. It was the complete opposite. I wasn't a toy for his use. I felt like a treasured gift.

By the time the calendar notification comes in for my meeting, I've failed to distract myself. I knock on Jeff's open office door that reads *Executive Director*. At the sound of my knock, he looks up from this computer and smiles. "Hey, Ren, come on in."

Before I sit across from him at his desk, I realize he doesn't have a copy of my report printed out like he usually does for our debriefs. I hold off on sitting, saying, "Oh, would you like me to make you a copy—or here, you can have mine." I offer my stapled packet and anxiously laugh. "It's not like I don't know what it says."

"Thank you." He takes it but doesn't spare it a single glance, setting it face down on his desk. "Listen, Ren . . ." He proceeds to explain that my position in the Development Office is being eliminated and all fundraising events will now be run through the Office of Special Events.

I don't let on that I know. I don't want Eliana getting in trouble for breaking confidence. Even though I knew it was coming, I still feel sucker punched. It doesn't sound like it has anything to do with my performance, but how can it not feel personal when I'm the *person* getting fired?

As I stand, he tries to apologize. Thank God for years of conditioning because despite feeling totally dejected, I'm able to politely smile and effuse, "Oh, it's okay, no problem at all, thanks."

I walk out of his office, finally processing that I no longer have a job. This is in fact a problem. A very big one.

Why did I just thank *him for firing me?*

I return to my office and sit down, staring blankly at my computer. After a few minutes, Eliana slinks in with a look that is part apologetic, part guilty, and part forced optimism. In her hands is a cardboard file box.

"Where did you find that?" I ask, perplexed. This is a scene straight from a movie.

"Charles gave it to me." Her intonation goes up like it's a question.

I explain, "I swear the only time I've ever seen a box like that is in movies when someone gets fired—you know, they shove picture frames and fake plants into it for their walk of shame through the office. I've worked here for four years and have never seen one until now."

"Why is that what you're worried about?" She pushes her thick, curly hair out of her face.

I laugh pitifully. "Hey, at least I don't have to risk running into Lewis everyday."

"This is so unfair." She huffs but begins to gather my small collection of fake plants dotting the office. She sets one in the box and gives me a look of support. "And I'm not letting you do this so-called walk of shame alone."

Thirty minutes later, Eliana and I are stepping out into the noon sun, my stupid movie-prop box filled to the brim. It feels surreal.

She gives me a hug as best she can with the box still in my arms and promises to call me when she "murders Jeff and/or Lewis."

I genuinely laugh, followed by a wave of bittersweet. "I'll miss you."

"What are you talking about? We're still going to see each other all the time—you're not getting rid of me that easily."

Eliana and I met through work but have become really good friends. I'll miss seeing her every day and hope that our friendship doesn't fizzle out without that daily connection. But I'm not optimistic.

Once she goes back inside, I make my way to my car and sit in the driver's seat.

What the hell am I supposed to do now?

It's ten days until Christmas, so the only people hiring are seasonal retail jobs. My parents would probably tell me not to even think about getting another job right away. They'd say something about returning to Mother Earth and listening for her guidance, to follow the sunbursts of my soul—*whatever the fuck that means.*

The first part of their assumed advice isn't that bad. I have enough savings that I don't need to rush into another job. But the idea of dipping into the rainy-day fund that I've meticulously grown gives me hives, even though I know it's for situations exactly like this.

That's the problem with growing up in a hippie commune bordering on a cult. My parents were, and still are, so free-spirited that I became the complete opposite for some semblance of control and ability to function in the real world.

When your parents give all their spare money to community living, budgeting every paycheck to the penny becomes a coping mechanism. When your parents bounced from job to job, sometimes solely relying on selling folk art at a roadside fruit stand, you get a degree in accounting because at least then you'll always have a job.

Well, look how well that turned out for me.

I startle when my phone rings and curse when I realize it's somewhere at the bottom of the box. I dig through my stuff without great care, trying to reach it before it goes to voicemail.

It's a number I don't recognize. "Hello?"

"Honey bear, it's Mama." Her voice has gotten raspier with age, but it's still a soothing coo. Every sentence she speaks sounds like she's reading a bedtime story.

"Mom? Is everything alright?"

"Of course, beary boo, why wouldn't it be?"

I may call her Mom, but I've always felt more like the parent. "Because you're calling me from an unknown number. What happened to your phone?"

"Oh, that." She laughs, the sound both comforting and aggravating. She provided a life based on seeking joy in the mundane, but she would also laugh when all I wanted was for her to take a single thing seriously. "I seem to have misplaced it. I'm borrowing Celeste's."

"Again? I bought you that one less than a month ago—"

"Well, I don't know why you did. I have little use for one on the ranch—that's why I'm always losing them."

I hold back an aggrieved sigh. We've had this conversation so many times, it's exhausting. "Because I need to be able to reach you or Dad in case of emergencies. What if I got in a car wreck? I could be dead for a week before anyone gets a hold of you."

"Oh, nothing like that is going to happen to you, honey bear. The Great Divine will protect you."

I pinch the bridge of my nose, attempting a calming inhale before continuing. "What did you call for, Mom?"

"I just wanted to hear your voice, sweetie." I wait silently for her real reason. After a beat, she continues, "And to let you know that your father and I won't be able to make it to the city for Christmas."

"*What?*" My heart sinks. They may annoy the hell out of me and have the technological skills of neanderthals, but I still love them dearly and was looking forward to seeing them. Especially now that every other part of my life is crumbling around me. "We've had this planned since before Harmony left."

I find myself fighting back tears. Since my sister, Harmony, has been a student at June Harbor University, she's been spending the holidays with me in the city, but a few months ago, she left for the Peace Corps. My parents offered to come so I wasn't alone on Christmas.

My bottom lip wobbles as I ask, "Why?"

"It's Popeye," she says solemnly. Of course this would be about one of the commune's barn cats. "We think the coyotes got him. No one's seen him in days. Everyone's rocked. It would be an insensitive time to leave when the family is suffering."

Of course the family she is referring to doesn't include me.

"What about Lewis? Can't you spend Christmas with him?"

I simply can't handle answering that question right now, so I lie. "Hey, Mom, sorry about Popeye, but my boss is calling me. I have to go."

"Alright, hon, love you." I can hear her smile through the phone, oblivious to my pain.

"Yeah, love ya too," I say quickly before hanging up.

I flop my head down on the steering wheel harder than intended, making the horn blare.

"*Fuck.*" I jolt upright and glance at the clock. It's barely past noon.

Eh, fuck it. I need a drink.

BAD IDEAS ONLY

Roman

"I'm pretty sure Harlow is wasted," Cash says with a laugh, looking up from his phone as we exit the car. The underground garage connects to their Irish pub, the Fox's Den. They live in the penthouse of the apartment complex above.

I smile internally. When she's drunk, she can't help gushing about Cash as a father. Stories that I love to hear, but ones that the boss of the most dangerous crime syndicate might not want to be public knowledge.

Like last time, when she told us about the time he wore their baby daughter's tutu and pranced around with a pocket square like he was a ribbon dancer. Of course, the tutu was so small, he had to wear it around his neck like a frilly Elizabethan collar.

The stories—and watching his reactions—are not only entertaining, but they fill me with pride. Nothing has shaped the man more than the life and death of his father, a violent, cruel, yet deeply respected man. The things that made him a strong boss were also what made him a shitty father. Cash's whole life has been about filling the man's shoes. Since the moment he found out Harlow was pregnant, he became haunted by the very thing he strove for. Something he never gave much thought became his number one fear: can he be the boss his father was without also being the parent he was?

He never admitted it outright, but when someone entrusts the life and safety of their family to you, you become pretty close; you know their unspoken fears. I'm probably one of three people that know the *real* Cash Fox. I knew he wouldn't be anything like his father, and witnessing him realize that is an honor. I think those tutus and pocket squares heal the deeply wounded boy he once was and soften the hardened man he is.

We enter the pub through the back, and when Harlow sees us, she waves us over to the bar animatedly. There's something familiar about the blonde woman she's sitting with whose back is to us. My natural re-action is to start cataloging everything about her and assess if she's a threat—occupational hazard being head of security and Cash's second. I've learned to never underestimate anyone.

At Harlow's enthusiastic greeting, the woman turns around, and I stop in my tracks.[1] Two things happen at once. I realize instantly where I know her from, and I identify the threat—scratch that, two threats:

Forgetting my own goddamn name.

And falling head over fucking heels.

"Roman, what is it?" Cash's terse voice unfreezes me.

"Nothing," I say brusquely and continue, trying to ignore the unsteadiness a single glance from this woman created.

"Cash, Cash." Harlow grabs her husband's arm and pulls him into her conversation. "Wait, Ren, tell Cash that story with the zebras and the polar bears." She laughs.

Cash looks at Ren. "Good to see you again, Ren. I'm glad you decided to take us up on our offer for a drink."

"And then some." Harlow giggles.

---

1. Play "Crazy"—Ben Goldsmith through scene break

"I can see that." Cash chuckles. "How is the diabolical plotting going?"

I finally turn toward Ren, something I was avoiding, to find her already staring up at me.

My throat goes dry and tight. Just like that night on her knees, her blue eyes are slightly unfocused but beautiful and bright. When she blinks, her long, dark lashes brush her cheeks. Her full lips are slightly parted as if she forgot what she was going to say. My pulse quickens. *What was she going to say?*

"Oh wait, did you guys meet already?" Harlow asks.

I wet my bottom lip. "Briefly."

She presses her lips together in an embarrassed smile, like she only just now realized she got caught staring. My lip quirks.

"Hi," she says sheepishly, like she's in a daze, followed by a small, tipsy giggle. Blush colors her cheeks. *Is she remembering the same things I am?*

"Good to see you again, Ren," I say with all the nonchalance I *don't* feel and hold out my hand.

As she shakes it, she gives me a look that is both curious and teasing, like she knows I'm fronting. Her bashfulness turns coy. "You know, when you came in, I thought you looked familiar."

"I have one of those faces," I say.

"No, I definitely remember your hands—" Ren replies confidently, still shaking my hand, and Harlow nearly spits out her wine. Suddenly realizing the slip, she quickly clarifies, "I mean *face*."

"I was gonna say . . ." Harlow laughs and takes another sip.

Cash looks at me, eyes slightly narrowed, then a subtle smirk plays on his lips. *He knows.* He might not have known before, but now? He definitely knows.

I excuse myself to talk with Alfie, Harlow's security, at the other end of the bar.

There's nothing I need to say to him, but I couldn't stay there.

Not without acting on some very dangerous thoughts.

I think Ren is going to fall off her barstool when she stands up, but she manages to get to her feet without making it to the floor headfirst. My eyes immediately follow the fall of her long hair cascading down her back to the generous swell of her hips accentuated by a fitted skirt.

Not for the first time, I'm jealous of a man that doesn't exist. The one I imagine waiting for her at home. The one that would get to listen to her laugh while she drunkenly recaps the night would get to peel that tight skirt off and kiss every inch of her skin. I can't imagine the kind of idiot that gave all that up.

Despite being parked in the back, I walk out the front entrance with the three of them. Even though I spent the night pretending she wasn't there, I can't deny myself just a few moments with her.

Outside on the sidewalk, we say goodbye. Harlow and Cash go one way, and Ren goes the other on her own.

My car is out back. My car is out back. My car is— She shouldn't be walking home alone.

She's wasted, and it's late. I'll hang back and just make sure she gets there safely. It's the right thing to do. That's it. Simple.

I follow from a distance for a block or two, noticing how the streetlights make her hair coppery.

What the hell am I doing? Not my circus, not my monkeys.

I'm about to turn around when a car with an illuminated ride share sign comes to a sudden stop and two fratty-looking finance bros stumble out. Not including the Fox's Den, there are two other bars they could be heading to, and half a dozen apartment buildings and townhouses. But something doesn't sit right with me.[2]

I'm a man of reason, and I learned a long time ago that trusting my gut is the most rational thing I can do.

I always hope to be proven wrong. Sometimes that does happen, but tonight isn't one of them.

The pair of men fall into stride behind her, their drunken demeanor shifting into a predatory prowl. Like a couple of jackals—spineless, opportunistic creatures who prey on the vulnerable. Not like the lion who goes after the buffalo—a fair fight. There's nothing more pathetic than a man who only goes looking for fights he can win.

They make a rowdy remark. I don't make out the words of it, but I can tell the message by their tone and the unease behind Ren's forced smile when she looks over her shoulder. I fight the burning urge to tell them to fuck off.

---

2. Pause "Crazy"—Ben Goldsmith

Just hang back, make sure she's safe. That's it. Nothing more, nothing less.

She picks up her pace, which accentuates what was only a slight drunken sway before. Then her foot catches where a brick is missing in the sidewalk and she tumbles forward, and my heart lodges in my throat. She lands on her hands and knees. The guys laugh as they hurry to help her up.

Just hang back, make sure she's safe, I remind myself yet again as their hands on her make me see red.

Only, they don't let go of her once she's back on her feet. They pull her toward an alley. And there's no fucking way I'm hanging back.

It takes me less than ten seconds to reach the mouth of the alley, and the pair are trying to coax her farther into the poorly lit and narrow passage, one on each side of her.

"So where are you headed?" One has his arm around her waist while the other has his arm linked with hers.

Before she even answers, one of them snickers. "Don't worry, we know a shortcut."

Her protests get more panicked but are still polite. "That's okay. I know where I'm going."

I wish more women were taught to kick men in the balls than be nice. God knows most of us deserve it every now and then.

But that's not our reality. So instead of being home in bed, I'm grabbing some punk by the back collar for a woman I have no business feeling this protective of.

"Hey—" the one I grabbed hollers as I yank him back and throw his ass down on the gravel.

"You two need to go. Right now," I say definitively. Ren looks back at me. My chest splits open at the relief that washes over her face when she sees me.

"Stay out of it, man." The one with his arm around her waist squeezes her tighter to his side. Her eyes get wide and scared as she tries to squirm away from the tight press to his body.

"Fuck, I think you broke my arm," the man on the ground whines, cradling his elbow.

"I haven't yet," I answer dryly. "But I will if you don't get the fuck up out of here."

"What the hell is your problem?" He rolls around like a baby or a male soccer player.

I ignore him, looking his partner in the eye so he knows that what I'm about to say is not an empty threat.

"And if you don't get your hands off her right this second, yours will be the arm I'm breaking."

As soon as he lets her go, all my attention is on Ren. I fight the burning desire to pull her to me. I want to clutch her face and make sure her eyes haven't lost their sparkle. My hands ball into fists at my sides so I don't while I make sure the men leave in my periphery.

She doesn't seem too shaken, and for that I'm grateful. In a selfish attempt to protect myself, I left her unguard-ed. I should have stepped in sooner. Nonetheless, I ask, "Are you okay?"

She nods with that same pleading look on her face she had that night, like she's begging me to take care of her, make her feel safe. And fuck if that isn't exactly what I want to do.

"I'm walking you the rest of the way home," I decide.

"No, no, it's okay. I'm fine." She averts her gaze and shakes her head, like she's embarrassed or it's a burden.

"That wasn't a question, Ren."

She spends most of the walk telling me funny animal stories from the zoo in what feels like one long run-on sentence. Almost like she's anxious about something. Do *I* make her nervous?[3]

When we get to her townhouse, she digs in her purse for her keys. After a minute of frantic searching, she just dumps the entire thing out on the stoop. "Shit." She sighs.

She looks up at me guiltily. "I think I lost my keys."

A lump forms in my throat. I should call our safe guy. If he can get into even the strongest vaults, he can get into her house. She should sleep in her own bed tonight.

It's clear what I *should* do.

Instead, I say, "Come on, you can crash at my place."

"Really?" She sounds shocked but excited.

I fight a smile, trying to keep my face neutral, and nod. I don't want her thinking *anything* is going to happen, not again and certainly not with her current level of intoxication. Though, I can't deny the fact that I would gladly get kneecapped if it meant *something* would happen.

"My hero," she practically shouts in singsong, grabbing me around the waist in an awkward side-hug.

---

3. Resume playing "Crazy"—Ben Goldsmith until end of chapter

Only, we're two steps apart, so I have to catch her from stumbling down the stairs.

I open the door to my apartment and step aside to let her go first, but she doesn't take the invitation. Instead, she looks up at me almost quizzically. If she's having second thoughts about spending the night, I wouldn't blame her.

I'm seconds away from suggesting we go back to the Den to look for her keys when she blurts out, "You're, like, *beautiful*."

I tilt my head. That was not what I was expecting.

"I mean, kinda old, but still really hot."

"Hmm," is all I say, fighting back a smile.

She gets a shy sort of amused quirk to her lips, like she can't believe she just said that out loud . . . but is happy she did. Then she swats my ass and skitters inside, giggling. I'm equally amused. I think the last time someone did that was high school baseball.

Suddenly, she spins around, her face fallen. "Wait, are you married?" Before I have a chance, she answers for me, "Probably. That's apparently my type."

"Excuse me?" My brows rise. "Do you think I would have done the things I did to you if I were married?"

"My boyfriend would." She scoffs, then continues to explain in that roundabout way drunk people do. "Well, *ex*-boyfriend. Emphasis on the ex. But you already know that. What you don't know is that I actually thought he was gonna propose that night. Can you believe that? His wife seemed really sweet though."

She looks at me expectantly.

"Not married," I clarify, stepping up to her. She tilts her head back to look up at me.

"That's good," she says like she's trying to hold back how happy that makes her.

It stings knowing I won't be able to continue making her happy like that. Something I quickly forget when she stretches up on her tiptoes, lusty gaze bouncing between my eyes and mouth. Before I know it, I'm grabbing her face and crashing my lips down on hers.

She moans softly and the sound shakes me to my senses. I step away, holding her shoulders. She looks dazed and a little giddy, brushing her fingers over her lips.

"Uh—" I clear my throat and swallow, trying to regain control of my heart rate. "You—I mean, I should go to bed. Let me show you to the guest room."

"Yeah, good idea." She forces a smile, and I hate myself for the embarrassed look that's now on her face.

She follows me, and it's different hearing another person's footsteps in my apartment. I'm not home often, and when I am, it's rarely with other people—especially not at this time of night. I had one woman sleep over a few months after Cass left, but quickly decided that was a bad idea. It's not fair to drag another woman into a promise I can't keep.

My job will always come first, and there's no point pretending any different.

"There's a bathroom in there." I point to a door on the opposite wall, then grab a fresh towel from the closet and hand it to her. "If you need one, I think there's a charger in the nightstand."

"Thank you," she says softly, getting a sleepy look, and I realize the blue in her eyes has a hint of green. Her fingertips brush mine as she takes the towel, and I get another strong, undeniable message from my gut.

Bringing her here was a bad, bad idea.

HANGOVER CURE

Ren

I wake up to what I'm certain are hundreds of tiny gnomes trying to pickax their way out of my skull. I keep my eyes shut as I roll over, refusing to make it any worse. The cool silk on this side of the pillowcase provides the tiniest bit of relief—*silk?*

I don't own silk pillowcases.

My eyes fly open, and I wince at the sun streaming through giant windows that I don't recognize. As I take in the unfamiliar setting, the previous night trickles back to me.

Was I really at the Fox's Den all day?

After the call with my mother left me in desperate need for a drink, I remembered Harlow's offer in the giraffe barn. I recognized the pub's name when they mentioned it because it's only a few blocks from my home and across the street from June Bug. I drove straight there, figuring I'd get a beer with lunch then drive home to contemplate my increasingly collapsing life.

Instead, I had a beer with lunch, then a few more when Harlow joined me, then switched to wine with dinner and afterward, until I finally left. There was no way I was getting behind the wheel of a car, so I decided to walk.

I don't remember how or when they showed up, but suddenly, there were two men on either side of me. I was confused and a little uneasy, but I think I was too drunk to truly process the danger I was in. Even now, my memory isn't crystal clear.

Mostly, what I remember is the flicker of the old streetlamp that grew fainter the deeper into the alley the two strangers pulled me. And Roman . . . *Oh my god, Roman!*

I clutch my breath as if I'm hiding from someone, except it's only my own mortification.

After sharing one night of the best not-sex sex of my life, I'm now the sloppy drunk girl who got too wasted to get home safely or keep track of her keys. I wish I could shrivel up under this comforter and disappear. Better yet, I should just leave. If I'm lucky, he'll still be asleep and I can sneak out. My phone tells me it's a little past eight, so I'll have to call a locksmith since the Den won't be open for another few hours. It will be worth it if it means I can get out of here without having to face Roman.

I slip out of bed still in my clothes from last night—*ew*—and look for my shoes. I find them on the floor with my purse halfway from the door to the bed. They're staggered in a line as if I stepped out of them while walking. *Adds up.*

My hopes for quietly sneaking out are quickly dashed when the first thing I see upon opening the bedroom door is Roman reading on the couch. He uses one large hand to hold the hardcover book with ease. His other hand sits around his mug, balancing on the armrest. He looks up as I exit the room and lowers his book. He doesn't say anything as he pins me with an unreadable look and slowly lifts the coffee to his lips.

After his sip, he just slightly tilts his head, still wordless. I feel naked under his silent, steady gaze. I even glance down to make sure I'm not pantless or something. When

I look back up, his dark brown eyes are still fixed on me, but he does *finally* say something.

"There are a few things for you on the counter." He nods toward the kitchen island behind me.

His apartment is spacious with an open floor plan and lots of natural light. It's modern and almost unnervingly clean, like something from a magazine. Looking around, I see there's almost no personal touch or items, even down to the undecorated Christmas tree.

"Thanks." I add to fill the silence, "So, you're one of those people that waits until the last minute to decorate their tree, huh? By Black Friday, my house is covered in tinsel and holly."

"I don't decorate it," he states flatly.

"What?" I practically gasp. "But the whole point of getting a Christmas tree is to decorate it." When he doesn't offer any explanation, I awkwardly turn toward the kitchen.

On the counter, I find a neat row of a bottle of ibuprofen, a glass of water, an iced coffee, and . . . "My keys!" I spin around, shocked. "Where did you find them?"

He sets his book down. "Last night, I called the Den, and someone had found them on the floor. After you went to bed, I went back to pick them up."

"Wow, thank you. That was really nice of you. I thought I was gonna have to call a locksmith."

My stomach swoops. The line of hangover remedies was thoughtful on its own, but offering me his guest room then going back out to get my keys is . . . straight up *erotic*. I'm tempted to get naked. I mean, if I already feel naked, then why not? Then I remember the way he sent me to bed right after kissing me. He probably wants me to get *out*, not naked.

"It's not a problem," he says dryly, then picks his book back up, and my stomach swoops again but not in a good way. He wasn't being extra thoughtful for my sake. He just doesn't want me to continue taking up more of his time. I've clearly ruined whatever he found attractive in me with my drunken carelessness of last night.

"Well, thank you anyway." I quickly swiping up my keys and throwing them in my purse. Just get me out of here before this situation gets any more embarrassing.

Unfortunately, I'm not that lucky, because seeing the front door makes me remember that I slapped his butt right before I walked in. Oh. My. God.

I try to will myself to spontaneously combust.

"The coffee is for you too," he offers without looking up from his book.

"Oh, thanks," I reply, a little perplexed. Picking it up, I recognize June Bug's logo—a man of habit. I walk to the front door as quickly as I can without being too obvious I'm running away with my tail tucked between my legs.

I open the door then uncomfortably throw out, "Okay, um, bye then. Thanks again."

His eyes flick from his book to me and the smallest hint of a smile tugs at the corner of his lips. "Anytime, vanilla iced latte."

His words shock me to my core. I'm so stunned that all I think to do as I run out the door is shout, "Sorry I slapped your butt!"

Before it closes, I swear I hear a chuckle.

VANILLA ICED LATTES

Roman

I wasn't always a coffee person.

Three months ago, I'd spent all night at the docks waiting for a delayed shipment. I'd been running on fumes by morning, so I'd gone to June Bug Café, right across the street, before reporting to Cash.

Three months ago, the barista had called out *vanilla iced latte* and the most beautiful woman I'd ever seen picked up the drink.

Three months ago, I became a coffee person.

And two days ago, I became irrevocably ruined when that same woman told me she wanted to be bad.

Ren

I feel like I'm in a walking dream as I head to the elevator. I press the call button. *Vanilla iced latte.*

But at the zoo, he acted like he didn't recognize me, when clearly that wasn't the case.

I hear the cables whir as the elevator climbs to my floor. *Vanilla iced latte.*

It opens slowly, and I step inside.

I hold the cold plastic cup to my burning cheek. *Vanilla iced latte.*

I feel giddiness I haven't felt in . . . *ever?*

The doors close, and I scream into the empty car, "*Vanilla iced fucking latte!*"

IS IT FAITH, OR IS IT DELUSION?

Ren

I plan on sleeping in the next morning—I mean, when was the last time I got to sleep in on a Tuesday? But then, even without an alarm, I end up waking up at the same time I would for work. I spent most of yesterday nursing my hangover and contemplating what it meant that Roman knew my coffee order.

Because here's the thing. He never gave me any clue, *either* night, that he recognized me from June Bug too. And he acted so disinterested yesterday. Granted, I did tell him at the zoo it would only be one time—something I am beginning to regret—and then made a drunken, butt-slapping fool of myself.

But then, he not only knew my coffee order, but had one waiting for me when I woke up after unexpectedly crashing at his place after an utterly embarrassing night.

Maybe he got it because he was going for himself and figured why not. Maybe he's just a keen observer and knows all the regulars' orders.

Maybe, maybe, maybe.

Then I hear my mother's voice in my head. "There are no maybes when it comes to your dreams, honey bear. If you want it, you got it. You just have to take the first step, and the Great Divine will do the rest. How else do you think I ended up with your father?"

She'd say this whenever my sister or I were doubting ourselves, then she'd retell the story of how she met our father.

My mom prayed for her dream husband, someone who was kind and tall, who made her laugh, and had "eyes as blue as the ocean." Then one day, she was walking home when a quiet but desperate meow caught her attention. She looked up toward the sound to see a tiny orange kitten stuck in a tree.

He was too high for her to reach, so she tried coaxing him down with some beef jerky she had in her bag. When that didn't work, she was conflicted about what to do next. She couldn't get him down herself, but if she went home to call the fire department, he might try on his own and get hurt. And then a man, no more than a year or two older than her, turned the corner.

All she noticed about him at first was his height. He was tall, well over six feet, which meant he'd be able to reach the kitten no problem. She asked him for help, and he quickly agreed. He got him down, and as he pet his little orange body, he said, "I was never any good at basketball, but I could go pro when it comes to rescuing kittens."

My mom laughed, and he looked up with a smile. It was then she noticed his eyes. They were ocean blue.

She asked if he wanted to come with her to the animal shelter. He thought for a second then said, "I don't know. He's a cute little guy. Maybe I'll keep him, that way I'll always be there to help when he gets stuck in trees." My mom laughed again.

Kind and tall, makes her laugh, and eyes as blue as the ocean.

She asked him out right then and there, and the rest is history.

When I was little, I loved listening to their story. It seemed like something out of a fairy tale. But as I got older, I realized that's exactly what it was, a fairy tale.

I sit up in bed. For so long, I've believed my parents are living in a rose-tinted world, that it's delusional to think that anything but hard work and smart planning is how you get where you want to be.

But I did everything *right* according to the rules of the "real world." Since I was a kid, I wanted to work with gorillas, but that was a foolish pipe dream. So instead, I got an accounting degree because that was the right thing to do, and hey, I still ended up working at a zoo. And working with gorillas . . . They were just made out of wire and Christmas lights.

I dated the guy I was supposed to date, the smart, successful one. Sure, he could be a condescending jerk sometimes, but that comes with the territory when you're at the top of your field, right? Turns out being a cheating bastard also comes with it.

Maybe my mom was right after all. Maybe I've been taking steps in all the wrong directions if they led me here, jobless and heartbroken.

Maybe the only reason I said "no numbers, no strings" was because that's what I thought I should do fresh out of a breakup.

Maybe, maybe, maybe.

Maybe it's time I borrow her rose-tinted glasses and take a step toward what I actually want, not what I *should* want.

I don't know if it's faith or delusion, but thirty minutes later, I'm walking into June Bug Café with my heart beating out of my chest.[1]

I step inside and unbutton my long coat. The shop is always a little on the hot side, but I never mind. The smell of fresh beans makes the warmth cozy, especially in the winter.

I do my best to discreetly scan the room, but like usual, I'm instantly drawn to Roman. Then I realize that for the first time, I don't care if it's obvious I'm looking around for him. He's sitting at a small circular table for two, the newspaper in his hands.

---

1. Play "Calm Me"—Vin Bogart

We spot each other, and my pulse stutters. He offers a small nod in acknowledgment, then returns to his paper. I debate for a few seconds whether to go right to him or order first. But then the decision is made for me when he folds up the paper and stands up like he's ready to leave.

If you want it, you got it. You just have to take the first step, I tell myself as I push down every insecurity and circling thought and walk over to his table.

By the time I reach him, he's shrugging on his coat. I catch a hint of his intoxicating cologne. It's rich and sensual and makes me want to squeeze my thighs together.

"Hey, are you leaving?" I ask, keeping my tone light and casual.

He meets my eyes and for a second, I think he's going to sit back down. Then his brow furrows just the tiniest bit like he's conflicted, and he says, "Yeah, you can have my table."

I wave my hand. "Oh, that's not—"

"It was good running into you, Ren. I'm sure I'll see you around," he dismisses as if in a hurry but trying to be polite.

He steps around me. My window is closing. I call out, "Actually, I wanted to thank you."

When he turns around, his eyes start at my feet and travel up my body while he drags his lip between his teeth. Chills run up my back in sync with his gaze. His attention is the headiest thing in the world.

He has that same conflicted look as he casually shakes his head. "It was nothing. Don't worry about it."

"And—" I begin, but he's already halfway to the door before I can say what I really wanted to.

Through the snowscape painted on the café's front windows, I watch him walk across the street to meet Cash outside the Fox's Den. I sit down with this odd feeling in my gut.

He was clearly meeting up with Cash at this time, but why does it feel like he was running away from me?

Could I be imagining that? Because I'm certain I didn't imagine the heated way he raked my body with his gaze.

I exhale, confused though not yet discouraged, and flip over the newspaper he left on the table. Two familiar faces stare back at me from mug shots on the front page. The headline makes my heart jump into my throat.

Two Arrested for Sexual Assault, Suspects in at Least Eight More Attacks, Police Say.

DUMBASS

Roman

I'm an asshole.[1]

A giant fucking asshole, I tell myself as Cash unlocks the Den. I knew what she wanted to ask, but instead of doing the right thing and turning her down once and for all, I hightailed it out of there like a goddamn coward.

The Den isn't just a pub. It also serves as the Fox family headquarters. Cash has an office in the back, but since the place hasn't opened yet, we just take the corner booth.

---

1. Continue playing "Calm Me"—Vin Bogart

I should have just kept up the ruse that I didn't recognize her outside of the gala, but then I had to go and buy that damn vanilla iced latte. I guess a selfish part of me wanted her to know that she wasn't mistaken, that I more than just recognized her. That I can't stop thinking about her. And it's only gotten worse since she's been in my home. I can't stop feeling like something is now missing.

Even now, I'm only half-listening to Cash as he rolls out a floor plan because her scent still lingers on my jacket where she hugged me. He points to two exits. "These are gonna be our weak spots."

A sharp rap at the window has us both instinctually reaching for our guns. Cash relaxes when he sees who it is. I look over my shoulder. Unlike him, I only grow tenser.

Ren is standing outside, waving the front page of the newspaper. Cash stands up, giving me a pointed look. "Don't be a dick," he warns before heading to let her in.

My pulse hammers as I listen to their friendly chatting grow closer and closer. Fuck, I'd be more at ease being shot at. I find my nerves around this woman appalling. I'm in dangerous situations almost daily, life-threatening ones weekly, and yet this little blonde, no more than five-four, has me shaking in my boots.

"Roman, Ren wanted to show you something," Cash says, sliding into the booth, smiling smugly. He's one of the only people who can clock my discomfort.

She slaps the newspaper on the table, front page up. "Are these them? Are these the guys you protected me from?"

I hesitate. If she's asking me, it's because she isn't sure. If I lie, she'll have even less reason to thank me. "Yes."

"Well, then," she says matter-of-factly. "You have to let me thank you. That could have been me. I could have been number nine."

"Alright. You're welcome," I reply, and Cash shakes his head.

"No, I mean let me take you out to dinner to properly thank you for saving my ass."

Fuck, my cock jumps at just her talking about her ass. *This* is exactly why I can't let her.

The more time we spend together, the harder it will be to keep my distance, and I *have* to keep my distance. If I don't, I'll only end up hurting her more when I inevitably choose my job and the Foxes over her.

"That's not necessary." My chest aches at the thought, but I say it anyway. "I would have done it for anyone." Her smile falters. *Hurt her now to avoid hurting her worse later,* I tell myself. Then bring it home with, "Is that all?"

Her face falls. "Yeah. I guess that's all."

She turns to leave, and Cash leans across the table to whisper scoldingly, "What the hell was that shit?" My eyes jump to Ren to see if she heard. She didn't. Or if she did, it didn't make her turn around.

"What do you mean?" I whisper back, playing dumb.

"I know Niamh's got me chronically sleep-deprived, but I'm not an idiot. You think I didn't notice that you just started getting coffee every morning? And that your newfound caffeine craving just *happens* to align with the same time a certain blonde gets *her* coffee?"

"I don't know what you're talking about—"

"Cut the crap, Roman," he hisses.

I sigh and begrudgingly admit, "Fine. And I didn't *just* start. It's been like, I don't know, three months or something."

He rolls his eyes. "Please, like you don't know the exact date and time you first saw her."

I throw my hands up in defeat and quietly shout, "Fine!" I fall back in the seat and cross my arms.

He smirks smugly again. He looks one second away from saying, *that's what I thought.* I close my eyes and massage both my temples with one hand. I listen to the heavy front door open.

"Wait, Ren!" Cash hollers, and I bolt upright. I cut him a glare, and he just smiles before waving her over. "Come back."

My heart pounds as she walks back over, looking unsure.

She stops in front of our table, her eyes nervously darting between the two of us. ". . . Yeah?"

"He'll pick you up at six," Cash says with a slick grin.

She eyes him skeptically. "What?"

"My friend here is being a dumbass, but he, in fact, likes you—quite a lot actually—and would love to have dinner with you." He leans back, looking disgustingly pleased with himself. "So, he'll pick you up tonight at six."

"Um, okay." Her cheeks pinch as she fights back a smile. She looks at me. "Roman?"

"I'll see you at six." I try to keep it at that, but she still looks unsure, so I sigh and add, "And he's right—"

"That you are a dumbass," Cash cuts me off with a laugh.

I shake my head. "That I really would like to have dinner with you."

MORALS AND ETHICS

Ren

I put on one of my favorite podcasts as I get ready for dinner. Dinner with *Roman*. Who apparently, and I quote, "likes me quite a lot actually." My current level of giddiness makes post-vanilla latte giddiness feel like a trip to the dentist. And I hate the dentist.

Which is one of the reasons I put on the video podcast in the first place, something to distract me from checking the time every two minutes. The show is two best friends who live across the country from each other just yapping. I feel like a fly on the wall for their weekly catch-ups and often aimless chatting.

I'm loosely curling my hair while Kelcie tells Autumn about a new guy she's seeing who she met on an app for people interested in kink. He had something called free use in his bio, so she asked him about it.

"So it's basically a mutually agreed arrangement where one partner can *use* the other whenever, wherever they want," Kelcie explains.

"What if I want to use them to do my taxes?" Autumn deadpans.

"No, like sexually." She laughs. "They can initiate sex without asking or foreplay and it doesn't matter if the other person is busy with something or asleep or whatever."

"*Asleep?*" I share Autumn's shock.

"Mm-hmm. I mean, that's somno, but it's included in a lot of free use kink. Like, imagine waking up and he's just inside you because he woke up in the middle of the night wanting you so bad," Kelcie says with an eyebrow wiggle.

Autumn sits back, looking scandalized, then admits, "Okay, that's hot."

"*Right?* And of course specific limits and boundaries are decided ahead of time, so sleeping or in public could be a hard limit previously established."

"Can they say no?" Autumn asks.

"Yes!" Kelcie says emphatically. "You're preemptively consenting to anything within your limits, but when it comes down to it, you always have the right to refuse."

"So you're basically agreeing to almost never saying no, but you still can."

"Exactly," Kelcie says. "And agreeing that they don't really have to ask."

"So I could be reading and getting fucked at the same time?" Autumn asks, interest piqued.

Kelcie shrugs with a smile. "I suppose so."

Autumn sits up and claps. "Great, where do I sign up?"

Kelcie laughs and says, "I'll tell you. But after a word from our sponsor . . ." I mute the show as it cuts to an ad.

My stomach swirls with mixed emotions. It feels like they just described my relationship with Lewis except without the prior discussion, agreement, or pleasure. Then finding out he was married the whole time . . . Yeah, I definitely feel *used*.

But then I think about the blunt and direct orders Roman gave me. How it made me feel to not only follow them, but see his appreciation when I did. I've never agreed with something so quickly as when he said *this pussy is mine tonight.*

My doorbell rings, and my heart skips a beat. I quickly shake out my hair and unplug the curling iron, butterflies beating up a storm in my stomach. As I make my way to the door, I can't help but wonder: what would it feel like to be willingly, *knowingly*, used by someone like Roman?

I take one deep breath before opening the door. Roman looks up from his feet when I do. He looks stunned, almost as if he expected someone else.

He runs his palm over his mouth as his eyes travel up and down my body. My chest pounds, giddiness turning to nerves. It feels like hours, not seconds, before he speaks.

"*Christ, Ren.*" He shakes his head with a heavy exhale.

I twiddle with the zipper on my clutch. "Is everything okay?"

His eyes widen as if he just realized how his reaction must look from my side. Then he says with a soft, sincere smile, "Yes. More than okay. You look great." My nerves melt away, replaced with glowing warmth.

"Well, you look . . ." I pause, taking in his long-sleeve knit with a raw hem and boatneck line that shows off the top of his toned traps and his charcoal tweed pants.

"Kinda old, but still really hot?" he offers with a mischievous tilt of his brow.

I cover my eyes with an embarrassed laugh. "Any chance you'll forget I ever said that?" I ask while walking out onto the stoop.

"The kinda old part? Sure." He places his hand on the small of my back as we walk down the steps, and I have to remind myself to breathe.

He opens the passenger door to a black Mercedes parked along the curb.

"The really hot part?" he says as I slip into the car, then before he closes the door with a smirk, adds, "Not a chance."

Roman

The server drops off our after-dinner sherry in petite glasses while Ren finishes telling me about her current job situation.

I thank him, then say to her, "It's really none of my business, but I think you made the right decision to take some time off before jumping into another job. And who knows? When you decide to start looking, maybe you'll find the perfect thing with gorillas."

"Yeah, maybe they'll need help balancing their accounts." I laugh. She takes a sip then asks, "And what about you and the Foxes? Friends or colleagues?"

I lean back in the leather booth and stretch one arm along the back. We're currently the only diners in the restaurant's back room. I drum on the upholstery, thinking about how I want to answer.

"Both," I end up saying. "But closer to family than friends."

"That must be nice. What do you do?" When I hesitate again, she jokes, "Unless it's classified or something?"

She's not far off.

Long before Cass ever left, I knew where it was heading. This job is what has always gotten in the way of any relationship, not that I've really been tempted these past twelve years. Until now.

I consider skirting around the truth, but similar to this morning when I considered lying to her about the men in the newspaper, it feels wrong. I decide to keep it simple and just be honest.

"What do you know about the Foxes?" I ask.

"Not a whole lot. The gala was the first time I met them, and they told me I could come by the Den anytime for a drink and to plan Lewis's demise."

"That definitely sounds like Harlow." I chuckle. "The Den is one of several establishments they own in the city. But they, the family, have many other business interests." My heart rate picks up. If I tell her this, there's no taking it back. I could tell her and she could walk out right now and I'd never see her again. My selfishness tells me to leave it at that.

But then she tilts her head and looks at me with those trusting eyes that only see the good in me and I know what I have to do. I swallow the knot in my throat and continue, "Many of which aren't legal, and I don't mean in the grey area or the unethical-but-legal arena." I trail off to gauge her reaction and see what conclusions she'll draw with only that information.

She purses her lips as she thinks and takes a slow sip of sherry. "Are we talking insider trading or like . . . the mob?"

"The latter." She nods slowly, taking in my answer, so I decide to add, "And occasionally the former." *Might as well get it all out there now.*

"Hmm," is all she says, and I feel my chest tightening, my fingers itching to reach for her wrist, feeling like she's going to run out of here any second.

"I'll answer any questions I can."

She thinks about my offer for a moment, then asks, "How did you go from special forces to the mob?" It's a fair question. I told her a little about my previous military career earlier.

"There were several things that happened to land where I did, but I don't think you're asking about a timeline of events. You want to know how personally, *morally*, I could go from patriotic soldier to criminal."

She nods, so I continue, "Well, like I said, there wasn't just one thing. It was a series of events, a . . ." I struggle to find the simplest explanation for something that is so complicated and layered. "A culmination of experiences that ultimately made me realize that, at least in this world," I say, referring to the criminal underground, "I always know who the good guys and bad guys are."

"And in my world?" she asks thoughtfully, without any hint of judgment, making me feel like maybe different worlds doesn't have to mean separate.

"It's more grey than it seems. When I was in the military, we were supposed to be the 'good guys,' but it didn't always feel that way. It felt like we picked and chose when and for whom our morals applied. The world I operate in now, it's simpler. There's a strict moral code. It's the same for everyone, it's not situational, and if you don't follow it, well, there are consequences. No matter who you are."

She pauses for a moment to look me in the eye. Though, it doesn't feel like she's simply making eye contact. It feels like she's looking, *really* looking, assessing. It's hard to breathe while I wait for her to find whatever it is she's searching for.

My lungs finally fully expand when she says matter-of-factly, "Okay."

"Okay?"

"I mentioned my sister, Harmony, right?" Now it's my turn to wordlessly nod. "My full name isn't Ren. It's Serenity—well, technically . . ." She bobbles her head side to side with half an eye roll. "It's Serenity Aurora Divine Calloway."

"Is your sister Harmony Borealis?" I joke.

"*Yes.*" She gasps and gives me a look like *how did you know?*

"Oh, I was joking." Now, I feel like a total ass.

"Well, I'm not." She laughs, and the sound is so welcome. I was worried I offended her. "Harmony Borealis Divine Calloway. After hearing that, I'm sure it won't be a surprise that we grew up in a hippie commune, but really it bordered on a cult."

That actually does surprise me. Nothing that I've learned about her so far would make me think that. I lean forward, giving her space to continue but making sure she knows I'm listening.

"I watched the leaders tear families apart because one spouse began to question their teachings or drain people of their life savings. There was one girl I grew up with who had severe learning disabilities, but she worked ten times harder than everyone else and got into her dream college, only to learn her parents had been brainwashed into giving away her and her brothers' college money for the 'betterment of the community.'" She makes air quotes.

"In theory, we were a self-reliant community, but in reality, we weren't becoming more self-reliant. We were becoming more isolated and dependent."

She traces the rim of her glass and chews on her inner lip for a moment, looking down at the table in thought.

After she sighs once, she looks back up with something nostalgic or bittersweet in her eyes.

"I'm not saying everything about it was unethical, but a lot of it was. Unethical, but as far as I know, legal. I could spend years trying to explain what I experienced and you would still never *truly* understand. Just like I will never understand all your life experiences and the nuances within them. So, how could I possibly judge your choices?"

A lump forms in my throat. I think I so expected her to race out of here when I told her who and what I am, that I never even considered how I'd feel if she didn't. And fuck, does it make me feel . . .

Words remain twisted up in that lump in my throat. So, all I can think to do is take her hand like she took mine in the barn and bring it to my lips. I feel her physically relax as I press a light kiss to her palm.

"*But . . .*" She gently pulls it away with a coy smile. "The second you are no longer a good guy with me, I am out of here." She says it lightly, almost as a joke, but I know she's serious.

"I'd hope you would. I think you've had enough of the bad guys. And you certainly only deserve all the good."

She laughs and teases, "All the good guys?"

"No." I hook my arm around her waist and pull her across the seat next to me. "Only one."

She wets her bottom lip and looks up at me through her lashes. *So. Fucking. Beautiful.*

I tuck her hair behind her ear then cradle her jaw. She so naturally follows my lead, tilting her face up, eyes dropping to my mouth. Damn butterflies take flight in my stomach and—

"Thank you so much for dining with us tonight." The server seems to fucking appear out of thin air, dropping the bill on our table.

She practically leaps out of her seat to be the first to grab it. I don't fight her, instead relaxing back. Her face falls when she opens it, glancing up for the server, but he's already gone.

She turns to me accusatorily, holding up the receipt for the paid bill. "What is this?"

I shrug smugly.

She huffs, crossing her arms, and stares me down.

I rest my elbow on the back of the booth and dust my thumb across my lower lip.

Her glare narrows.

"*Yes?*" My brow lifts.

After a beat, a sly smile teases her lips. "Since you paid for dinner, I still have yet to properly thank you."

"Mm-hmm." I nod, curious where this is going.

She looks away bashfully but returns confident. "Have you heard of something called 'free use'?"

MAKING ARRANGEMENTS

Roman

R en concludes her frazzled explanation of free use kink with a big breath, as if she were holding hers the entire time. She presses her lips together and waits expectantly.

I know what free use is, not from any personal experience. In fact, everything I learned was against my will from Cash . . . and Niamh was born nine months later. I haven't given it much thought since then, no matter how interesting I found the concept, because there didn't seem to be any point. There was no one to practice it with, nor was I looking for someone. Until now.

"What exactly are you proposing, Ren?"[1] I have a pretty good idea, but she hasn't explicitly said.

So far, she's only asked me one thing: have I heard of free use. But how that relates to her thanking me . . . I want to hear her say it.

She gives me a pleading look, her cheeks burning pink, begging me not to make her spell it out.

She bobbles her head and whispers, "*You know . . .*"

"Do I?" I cant my head to the side. "Maybe I do, maybe I don't, or maybe I want to hear you say it." My hand finds its way to her thigh, and I spread out my fingers excruciatingly slowly as I continue, "Say that you want me to use you for my own pleasure. Say that your perfect little cunt is mine to lick or fuck or simply use to warm my cock. Whenever I want."

I glide my hand higher up her leg, over her dress. Her breathing grows shallow. My palm slides to her inner thigh, and she eases her legs apart. Her teeth bite into her lip with anticipation.

And then I stop. My fingertips an inch from her pussy. "I do need you to say it, Ren. And not just for my own desire to hear those filthy words off your lips, but

---

1. Play "Body"—Rosenfeld

because this can only work if you're able to articulate exactly what you want."

"You're right." She sits up taller. "I do want you to use me. I want to give you whatever you want to take." She reverses the words I said to her in the barn. She lifts her chin, gaining confidence. "I want to feel dirty and desired. Used and owned, but treasured."

I resist the urge to finish this conversation right here and make her feel as used and dirty as she's asking for. Instead, I ask, "How long until you consider me properly thanked?

"Hmm." She thinks. "How about until Christmas?"

It feels like so little, but at the same time, it's more than I ever expected to get with her. More than I ever thought I'd allow myself.

"Deal," I agree. "Which means that for the next five days, when you're awake, you're mine, but what about when you're asleep?"

I don't think she's aware of it, but at my question, she presses her legs together, bringing my hand closer yet to where she craves my touch the most.

Still, she gives it a moment of thought, which I appreciate. I want her going into this with her eyes wide open clear.

"Yours," she breathes.

My cock swells at the thought, slipping inside her wet cunt while she dozes peacefully, rocking into her slowly and gently so as not to wake her.

"But only if we go to bed together," she adds. "No sneaking in through my window"—her lips quirk—"*yet.*"

"And when we're in public?" I lightly drag my index finger up and down, just barely brushing the dress fabric over her pussy.

"Yes." She draws out the single syllable, then adds, "If-slash-when you think we can get away with it."

"Like a barn in the middle of a gala?" She nods, excitement in her eyes. My middle finger joins my index. "Or the empty back room of a restaurant?"

She inhales sharply when I apply a little more pressure so it's no longer just the fabric I'm brushing against. Then she exhales. "*Yes.*"

"So I could just pull you onto my lap." I mirror my words with action and instantly feel my control fray a little more with her ass now grinding against my cock.

"Yes," she says again, relaxing back into my chest as my hand splays wide over her plush stomach.

With my other hand, I brush the hair off her neck and dust my lips up her velvet soft skin. "Remember, you can always say *no* or *stop* and I will. Immediately. But I want another word, just for us, that you can say anytime, anywhere, and everything stops."

"I can't imagine ever wanting you to stop," she says breathlessly, a haze of lust already heavy in her voice.

I smile into her skin. "All the same, I want that word."

"Um, okay . . ." Both of my hands rest on her thighs and I slowly push them apart. "It's really hard to think when you're . . ."

"Touching you?"

"Yes."

"You're right. I'll stop—"

"*No*," she protests, and I chuckle.

"You didn't let me finish. I'll stop until you give me that word."

"Okay, okay," she says hurriedly. "What about giraffe?"

"Giraffe it is." I seal it with a soft kiss to her neck. "Now open your legs for me, sweet girl, and put them on either side of mine."

When she does, her ass cheeks hug my cock, making me quietly groan. She seems to melt at the sound and mumbles lustfully, "God, I want to feel you inside me."

"*Fuck,* sweet girl, you really are desperate to be used, huh?" She nods and rolls her hips in my lap teasingly. I clamp them still, my fingers digging into her full, round flesh. "That's too bad because I had other plans for you tonight."

I keep one hand firmly on her hip to remind her who's in control and the other disappears under her skirt. Her thighs are silky and warm, just the feel of them making my blood pump harder.

"I haven't been able to stop thinking about this needy pussy or the way you came for me so sweetly, drenching my fingers like a good fucking girl. I want you coming in my lap again, just like that."

"Um . . ." She hesitates. "I don't think you understand."

"What don't I understand?"

"That you can use me for your *own* pleasure." There's a hint of insecurity in her voice. I want to quash it immediately. I'm sure it took a lot of courage to bring up free use in the first place. I want her to keep that confidence.

"What *you* don't understand, Ren, is that making you come, getting to watch how my touch makes you fall apart . . . that *is* me using you for my own pleasure."

"Oh," she says, like the idea never occurred to her. That little stunned noise makes me want to destroy every man who made her feel like her pleasure didn't matter.

"Now, I'm going to finger fuck your perfect cunt, and the only thing that is going to stop me from making you come is your safeword."

"*Yes,*" she says with quick, short nods of her head.

I fight the instinct to praise her because even though I love the way she melts when I do, I want her to understand that saying yes isn't what makes her a good girl. It's her trust and honesty that do.

"And just so you know," I whisper in her ear, "the first time you take my cock, it won't be at some restaurant where I'm rushing just to get you home and fuck you properly."

My fingers find the lace of her panties and her breath hitches. "If I had known you were so eager to be used, I would have told you not to bother with these."

I stroke her swollen lips over her panties, getting even harder at the feel of the fabric dampening. "In fact, as much as I love the idea of you soaking your panties, from now on, when you're with me, you don't wear any."

"Okay." She nods, almost timidly.

I wonder if it's because she's uncertain of her answer or if, like before, she's simply distracted by my wandering fingers. So I pause and ask, "Do you like the sound of that? Always being ready for me to fill you anyway I choose? Always ready to be bent over and fucked filthy?"

I finally slip my fingers into her panties and stroke her slit. She shudders, her answer coming out in a shaky whisper. "Very much so."

"Good." I hum into her neck, then rake my teeth down it.

Finding her slick clit, I circle it with two fingers, and she arches into me. I lave my tongue over the pulse at the base of her neck then suck a bruise into the delicate skin. She moans. My cock jerks.

Fuck, maybe I really do want to bury my cock in her hungry little pussy right here after all.

But then her leg twitches, a quick jolt, and I know without a doubt that this is all I want to do. "God, you're so responsive."

She stiffens, sitting up a little off my chest. "I'm sorry."

I twist her in my lap so I can look her in the eyes. "What for?"

"Twitching, wriggling. Sometimes I just can't help—"

"Ren." I stop her right there. "I *love* that your body can't help but show me how you feel. Getting to learn what you like, what makes you feel good, is an honor."

Her eyes soften, and she places her hand on my cheek before pressing a light kiss to my lips and spinning back around so her back is to my chest.

"That's my girl," I murmur and slip back into her panties.

She trails her hands up and down my arms as I play with her clit. It's not long until her breath gets choppier and her moans sweeter, needier. She begins to rock into my touch, chasing her pleasure.

"That's a good girl. Keep riding my hand, baby," I encourage her, kissing her neck and nibbling on her earlobe.

"Oh, yes, yes," she mewls. Her legs start intermittently squeezing mine.

"Don't forget, this pussy belongs to me and only comes with my permission."

"O-okay." She nods, her body practically trembling in my arms.

I almost laugh when the waiter choses this moment to return for our glasses and she curses under her breath before thanking him with a quaking voice. When he leaves, she groans needily, every muscle in her body tensing.

I don't hide the teasing in my tone. "Is there something you want to ask me, Ren?"

"Can I—*oh fuck*—" Her hips buck. "Can I come? Can I come, *please?*"

"*Hmm.*" I delay answering her, and she whimpers. She really is trying so hard. She holds her breath. "Yes, come for me."

She exhales and shatters. Her hands clamp down on my arms and her back arches. "Oh my *god.*"

The way she melts in my arms after fills me with pride and contentment. I try to focus on that instead of the hint of dread reminding me this is only for five days.

14

USED

Ren

He kisses me ravenously against his apartment door while fumbling to unlock it.[1] I grab either side of his face to pull him to me just as hungrily. When he tugs on my bottom lip with his teeth, my legs nearly give out.

When the door finally opens, I fall backward. He catches me and lifts me off the floor in one smooth movement. He never breaks the kiss as I wrap my legs around his waist, and he carries me to the kitchen island.

He sets me down and feverishly pushes up my dress. I spread my legs for him to step between them. At

---

1. Play "Potential"—BOBI ANDONOV

the same time, I'm clawing at his belt and tugging his tucked-in shirt. I feel like an uncoordinated mess of limbs, but I don't care. I just *want* him.

My palms slip under his shirt and slide up the hot, hard canvas of his abs as he shimmies off my panties. Out of the corner of my eye, I see him shove them into his back pocket.

He breaks our kiss to look down and watch his wide hands glide up my bare thighs. His thumb massages the crease between my leg and hip. It's a ticklish, intimate spot that makes me squirm then melt further into his touch.

My hand slips into his pants and wraps around his thick cock, making him fall forward with a delicious, throaty groan that sparks along my skin. His breath is hot on my neck as he rests the side of his head against mine. The way I make him fold with the smallest slide of my fist is a rush, making me more eager, if that's even possible.

"*Fuck*," he curses and goes from tempered, control movements to roughly hooking his arms under my knees and forcefully tugging me to the edge of the counter.

He holds my legs even wider. My heart races as I feel the cool air against my spread pussy. I feel exposed and manhandled and *hot*. So fucking hot, like I could burn up with just a fraction of his attention. He's so focused on me, like he's trying to commit every inch of my skin to memory.

I race to push his pants over his hips and free his cock. His fingers dig into my thighs as he rocks his pelvis forward, and I bring his tip to my center.

"Let me feel you," he rasps. Mouth watering and chest pounding, I drag his thick head through my slick folds.

I look down to watch. My breath hitches when it grazes over my clit. "*Oh, please.*"

He's not even inside of me, and it's the hottest fucking thing I've ever seen. I can't tear my eyes away.

Until I'm forced to. He wrenches my head back with a fistful of my hair. "This isn't about what you want," he growls. "This is about me owning this cunt for the next five days. And you better believe I'm going to use you like a fucking whore."

My pussy clenches. *Oh god, do I want that.*

Like I'm nothing more than a doll, he pulls me to my feet and spins me around so fast it takes my breath away.

He bends me over harshly, my cheek pressed into the cool marble.

His hand trails down my spine, making chills ripple down my arms. His cock rests on top of my ass, and I hear the distinct sound of tearing foil then feel him putting a condom on.

After he drags his cock back and forth over my pussy, his hips press tight against my bottom. He grabs my shoulder with one hand. His breath becomes slower, louder as he positions himself at my entrance. I bite my lip hard in anticipation.

He makes one strong thrust at the same time he pulls me back with the hand on my shoulder, sinking his cock deep inside me. I cry out at the sudden fullness, but it turns to a sharp moan as he rocks partially back and pistons forward again.

"*God*—" I sputter, my hands clawing for purchase at the edge of the counter.

"You look even better with my cock buried in this dripping pussy than I ever imagined."

He proceeds to fuck me with fast, powerful snaps of his hips. His thick cock drags against every sweet, oversensitized nerve inside me. The hard edge of the counter digs into my hips, and the bite of pain every time he brutally thrusts into me only adds to the feeling of being used.

I don't have to do anything but take it. It's blissfully overwhelming.

And becomes even more so when he reaches around to cup my pussy. The heel of his palm presses against my clit. The next time he pounds back in, my pussy grinds against it and I moan loudly.

"*Fuck—fuck—fuck.*" I mewl with every thrust. My toes curl in my heels, and my fingers wrapped around the counter edge ache with how tightly I'm gripping it. My lungs feel halved in size the higher and higher he works me.

"You are not to come," he orders coarsely.

"*What?*" I gasp, my clit already throbbing.

"You heard me. Don't you dare fucking come."

Surely, he knows what he's doing with his hand. He can't be serious. "But—"

"Do I need to gag you?" he snarls, and illicit fear races through me.

"Uh-uh," I mumble and clench my teeth together. When that doesn't stop the pleasure from flooding my blood, I try biting my tongue. I so badly want to do as he says, but—

"*I—can't—stop!*" I cry as everything crests and comes crashing down over me.

My pussy pulses around his cock as I come and my legs shake. The sound torn from me is unlike any noise I've made before. It's raw and desperate, pained yet drenched with ecstasy.

I feel like I'm caught in a rough tide, being rocked by waves, until I crash into a rock. Roman rips me off the counter and forces me to my knees. His hand tightly gripping my hair stills me.

"Your body doesn't belong to you anymore. It belongs to me, and I decide when you get to come and when you bite down and take it. So now, since you can't handle my cock in that greedy pussy, I'm going to have to use another one of your holes."

I swallow hard, my scalp stinging where he fists the top of my head. "Yes, I'm sorry—"

"Open," he cuts me off.

I drop my jaw, opening as wide as I can. He taps my cheek with his hard cock, covered in my juices. "There's my good girl. I knew you could follow instructions after all. Now relax your throat."

He drags his cock over my lips before taking the condom off. When I lick my lips, I can't help but moan at the salty taste on my tongue, knowing I'm tasting my own lust. He cocks one brow, his gaze smoldering as he slides into my mouth. "Do you like how you taste after being used?"

"*Mm-hmm,*" I hum the best I can with him filling my mouth.

"I'm not going to be gentle, sweet girl. Squeeze my thigh if it's too much." I blink slowly, acknowledging him. "But I know you can take it." The hint of a smile tugs loosely on his lips before he clenches his teeth together and shoves his cock to the back of my throat.

Instantly, my eyes water. My instinct is for my hands to fly to his thighs, but I resist it. I know I can do this, and knowing I have an out if needed gives me even more conviction. I ball my hands into fists in my lap and loosen my jaw and throat as he continues to fuck my face with powerful thrusts.

I look up to find his gaze already waiting for me. His eyes narrow, and a smirk flits across his mouth as our eyes lock. "That's it . . . *Fuck* . . . *Yes* . . ." His groans are deep and masculine, stroking something soft and primal inside me, the ultimate calming effect. Even as I choke and gag, his deep brown eyes stay with me, and anything that isn't me or him just fades away.

"God, Ren—fuck, fuck, f-f-fuck!" He grips the top of my hair with both hands and holds me still as he comes hot and heavy down my throat. He exhales raggedly, closing his eyes and rolling his head back, like he's been depleted of the strength to even hold his head up.

"*You*," he mumbles, and he slowly pulls his head back up, sliding out of my mouth. He gives me a lazy, sated smile. It warms me to my core.

"C'mere, sweet girl." I expect him to help me to my feet, but instead he bends down and completely scoops me up in his arms.

SENIOR DISCOUNTS

Roman

Her body is heaven.[1]

Every soft roll and curve. Every inch of her dimpled thighs and striped hips. The steam collecting in little droplets on her shoulders. Even the loose, sweaty strands that have fallen out of her bun and cling to her neck like rivers on a map.Play "Are You Even Real (feat. Givēon)"—Teddy Swims, GIVĒON through first scene break

A heaven I can hold as we sit in the bath together, her nuzzled between my legs with her back to my chest.

---

1. Play "Are You Even Real (feat. GIVĒON)"—Teddy Swims, GIVĒON through first scene break

I scoop up some water in my hands and run them down her arms. "How do you feel, beautiful?" I'm a little worried I may have been too harsh or rough.

"Good," she responds immediately, then sighs as if taking time to actually consider the question and adds, "Really good." I can hear the smile in her voice. "How do *you* feel?"

I take a moment to genuinely check in with myself, and the answer comes to me easily. "Lucky." She sighs happily and relaxes even more against my chest. "Did you feel safe the whole time?"

"Yes," she says instantly and sincerely, making the knot of worry in my chest loosen completely.

"What did you like most?"

"Hmm . . ." She rolls her head to the side, allowing me to see her cute *thinking* face. "The way you talked and the way you just, sorta . . . threw me around."

I chuckle. "That's good 'cause I very much enjoyed 'throwing you around.' Is there anything you didn't like or want more or less of?"

She looks down and lifts her stomach, straightening her legs as much as she can. She brushes over angry-looking red marks on the front of her hips.

"Jesus, did I do that?" I ask, horrified. She starts to respond, but of course I did. What a stupid fucking question. "I am so sorry. I probably should have started with that. Christ, I will be more gentle next time, or—or grab a pillow or something. *Fuck,* I am *so* sorry—"

"*Roman,*" she snaps, twisting so she can look me in the eye like I did at the restaurant. She puts her hand on my thigh and gives me a pleading, almost pitiful look. "Please don't."

"Don't what? Don't *apologize*? I absolutely should. I *hurt* you." She really needs to stop putting men's egos above her own needs. I'm going to give her some kickboxing lessons, I decide.

"Don't be gentle!" she says, exasperated.

I blink at her. "What?"

"I *like* them. I don't know. There's just . . . something hot about walking away from being fucked so hard there are bruises."

I audibly sigh louder than I think I ever have. "Oh."

She gives me a *yeah, dummy* smile. "You asked what I wanted more of, so I checked to see if the counter left a mark. And I'm *happy* it did because I wouldn't mind a few more of them, okay?"

I smile back and hug her tight to me. "Okay. Anything else? And I promise I won't interrupt before you finish."

She points at me with a flirty smirk. "Now, that's hot. And let me think . . ." She faces forward again and relaxes back into me. The fact that she seems so comfortable in my arms really has me feeling some type of way. "Can I get back to you on that?"

I kiss the top of her head and smile to myself. "Absolutely."

"What about you?"

"I'm still expecting to wake up from this dream."

The next morning, I am not surprised to find that my cock has woken up before me, wedged against Ren's ass, hard as a fucking rock. She moans sleepily and rocks back into me. One of my hands cups her breast, and I start lazily playing with her nipple. She moans again and rolls her head back, allowing me to press tender kisses to her neck.

"I definitely don't think I'd mind waking up to you inside me," she murmurs, and my cock jerks.

"I don't think I'd mind waking you up that way either," I mumble into her warm skin. "Though, having to get up for a condom kinda ruins the whole slow-morning aspect of it all."

"I know." She sighs, still grinding her ass leisurely against me. "I didn't expect you to agree to dinner so quickly, but I was planning on getting tested. When was your last clean test?"

"A while ago, but I haven't been with anyone since." A thought occurs to me. "Still, I could call the doc and have him come over. It never hurts to get checked again."

"The doc?" She rolls over to face me.

"Dr. Romero. He's one of the on-call doctors the Foxes have on retainer—but don't worry, everything would be completely private. Romero doesn't play when it comes to patient confidentiality, no matter how absurdly he gets paid."

She laughs. "I have a lot to learn about your world."

While we've been talking, I've been exploring her supple back. It was pretty absentminded until right now, when my hand gliding up the back of her leg slips between her thighs.

"Fuck, sweet girl, you're already soaked just *thinking* about being used, hmm?" She scrunches her nose and glances away. "Don't you dare be embarrassed, Ren. This, *you*—" I shake my head, in disbelief if I'm being honest. "So fucking hot."

She smiles dreamily. "Where did you come from?"

I chuckle. "Funny, I was just wondering the same thing about you. Now—" I roll her onto her back and chide, "Let a man eat, would ya."

Then I disappear under the sheets to the sound of her giggling.[2]

"Alright, thanks, Cash." I hang up with him and turn to Ren, who is walking out of my en suite, scrunching her hair with a towel. She's in one of my tees and a pair of pajama pants that are rolled at least four times at the waist and still nearly a foot too long. I point to her. "You—"

"Need a pair of scissors. How attached to these pants are you exactly?"

I chuckle. "What about some boxers?"

---

2. Stop playing "Are You Even Real (feat. GIVĒON)"—Teddy Swims, GIVĒON

"That'll do." She smiles like I just told her a really cute story instead of asking if she wanted to wear a pair of my underwear.

While I go to grab some, I continue what I was about to say. "You've made quite an impression on Cash. We were supposed to meet later, but when I told him you were here, he suddenly felt like rescheduling." She looks a little confused. "In the thirteen plus years I've worked with him, I can count on one hand the number of times he's rescheduled for something that wasn't a life-or-death situation."

"Oh." She nods and saunters over to where I'm leaning against my dresser, trying not to trip on the pant legs.

She tosses the towel in her hand into the laundry basket, and I pull her closer by the hips. I'm already dying to peel these clothes off and get right back in bed. I reach for her face, tilting it up to meet me as I dip down—

"Or he just feels bad that you don't have anyone to share your senior discounts with—*ow!*" She yelps when I slap her ass. Her expression of shock quickly melts into a smirk. "Do it again." Suddenly, the desire to be back in bed is completely gone. Right here will do just fine.

I step out from between her and the dresser, then fold her over. She catches herself with her hands, leaving her bent at the hips, ass out.

I grab her damp hair like a leash and bring my palm down, hard and fast on her full cheek. She lets out a sharp cry. I keep her head tugged back and lift my hand for another one when the doorbell rings. We both freeze.

"Shit. I could tell him to come back," I offer, and not a *little* desperately.

"No, no, it's okay." She stands up, and I release her hair. "I'd rather continue this when there won't be anything between us." She quirks her brow, making her meaning clear.

"*Fuck,*" I groan and roll my eyes to the ceiling and back. "Fine, but can you say that again?"

"Say what again?" she asks, pretending to be oblivious. She steps right up to my chest so she has to look up at me through her lashes. "Say that the next time you fuck me, there better not be anything in between us?"

I release a desperate sound that is half-sigh, half-growl and drag my bottom lip through my teeth. "Yeah, *that.*"

The doorbell rings again, this time accompanied by a loud knock. I hand her the boxers I pulled out and holler begrudgingly, "I'm coming!"

THEN COMES BABY IN A BABY CARRIAGE

Ren

We say goodbye to Dr. Romero. Not quite sure what I expected of an on-call mob doctor, but he was a perfectly pleasant man. It takes a special kind of person to make you not feel awkward handing over a little plastic cup of your pee, and I barely felt the needle when he drew blood. All in all, I'd give him five stars on Yelp.

Roman closes the door behind the doctor and turns to me.[1]

As if on cue, my stomach grumbles. He looks aghast. "You're starving. I need to get some food in you. I'm so

---

1. Play "I Feel Love"—Freya Ridings until indicated

sorry. I'm not a big breakfast person and forget others are."

I can't help but laugh at his deathly concern. "I'm hungry, not starving. No need to declare a state of emergency."

"Okay." He chuckles. "But can I please feed you? Soon, preferably."

"You may." His genuine desire to care for me makes it easy to accept. "Though, I might have to call bullshit."

His smile turns to a frown. "On what?"

I give him a flirty smirk. "Well, you definitely seemed like a breakfast person this morning."

He laughs with a smile that is completely uninhibited. And goddamn if it doesn't make me *weak*. Before these five days are over, I promise myself I'm going to get a photo of him smiling like this, a beauty that must be preserved for the sake of humanity . . . and myself.

He raises his hands in surrender. "I stand corrected. Now, where do you want to eat? The other thing about not being a breakfast person is not having any breakfast food on hand."

About three places immediately come to mind. "What about—did you put lights up?!" They're unplugged, so I didn't notice right away, but there is in fact a string of lights wrapping around his otherwise bare Christmas tree.

"Oh, yeah." He rubs the back of his neck and half-shrugs.

"I thought you don't decorate?"

"I don't." Then his eyes go up and down my body, and he smiles out of the corner of his mouth. "Or I *didn't*."

I resist the urge to jump up and down. "This is great news. I can help you put ornaments up later if you want."

He grimaces. "I don't have any—well, I have these, but I put them on and they just looked silly."

Walking over to the tree, he pulls out a box of frosted ornaments.

I laugh. "Well, of course they would. It's a seven-foot tree and you only have six."

"Now that I hear you say it." He chuckles, unembarrassed. "How about after eating, we go buy some more, the *proper* amount?"

I can't help but twist side to side excitedly. "I can't think of any other way I'd rather spend the day."

After the best breakfast sandwich of my life, we get back in Roman's car.

"So, where to?" he asks.

"I've been thinking about this. Most people have a collection of assorted ornaments that they've gathered over years and years. And that's one of the things that I love about Christmas trees. It's like a chronicle of a family's story, right?" He nods, following along. "But we're starting from scratch, and you don't want a boring tree with all these perfectly uniform ornaments. No offense or anything."

He huffs a small laugh. "Don't worry, none taken."

"Good." I smile then continue explaining, "So, I think in order to get that look, we should go to a thrift store. They're a treasure trove this time of year, and there's a huge one less than a mile from here."

"Done and done." He bobs his head, pleased. "Let's do it."

A few minutes later, we're walking into Thrift 'n Things. It's usually crazy this close to Christmas, but I guess a Thursday at eleven is slow even during the holidays. Apparently, a local nursing home figured the same thing.

Right after us, a dozen or so octogenarians stream in. A bus with the facility's name and smiling stock photo of an older couple waits outside for them. Roman and I watch them slowly disperse down the many aisles then look at each other.

I grin. "Oh good—"

"Don't," Roman warns playfully.

While trying not to laugh, I explain, "I was just gonna say—"

"That I could get a ride home with them?" He lifts his brow as if unamused, but I can tell he's fighting a smile.

"I was actually going to suggest we ask them about their water aerobics program."

Wholly unconvinced, he asks, "Oh really?"

"Yeah, really," I insist. "It's obvious how important staying in shape is to you." I bite down on my lip to keep it together, but all hope is lost when he cracks first and starts laughing.

He hooks one giant, muscular arm around my neck and pulls me into his chest. He kisses the top of my head then uses the same tone he does when fucking me to say, "Put your hand over your mouth."

I don't ask why. I do it immediately, without question.

Half a second later, I scream into my palm, my right ass cheek burning. If I were to lift up my dress right now, I'm certain there'd be a glowing red handprint.

I'm sure my eyes are as wide as saucers when I look up at him. His lip quirks and he has a satisfied, smug glint in his eyes. He presses his lips to my temple and whispers, "Better watch what you say while this fine ass belongs to me."

My heart beats wildly, adrenaline racing through me from the unexpected slap. My butt stings eight ways to Sunday, and yet, I find myself replying, "Don't tempt me with a good time, Gramps."

He relaxes his arm so it's loosely slung over my shoulder and laughs. "Let's go, Horny Hallmark."

"Horny Hallmark?!" I gasp in mock offense as we start toward the Christmas display. "At least Gramps is kinda cute."

He feigns innocence. "I thought we were just calling it as we see it." Then he tugs me a little closer and flashes me a quick, sweet smile.

We walk side by side, his arm wrapped comfortingly around me, to rows and rows of hooks loaded with ornaments and two big tubs labeled clearance.

It doesn't take long until our hands are full, six ornaments dangling from four of my fingers. A very helpful store clerk offers us a basket and we gratefully off-load them, then restart our treasure hunting.

One of the old ladies from the group shuffles past us then pauses and asks curiously, "Shopping for yourselves?"

"Yes, ma'am," Roman says, flashing a smile that has women of all ages swooning.

"Then don't bother getting that one. You'll be gifted at least five." She winks then continues on.

Roman and I look at each other, confused, then down at the ornament in his hand.

It's a pewter baby carriage with an embossed banner reading Baby's First Christmas.

"*Oooh*," we say simultaneously, then laugh.

"I was going for this one," he says and pulls the next ornament off the hook. A giraffe.

My stomach flutters. "I'm not a lawyer, but I'm pretty sure we're legally obligated to get that." I shrug like it truly is out of my control.

He nods in agreement, and I catch him smiling as he drops it into our basket.

"Do you have kids?" I blurt out and instantly regret it. This is supposed to be a fun, low-stakes five days. I immediately try to backpedal. "Is that too personal? Ah, never mind—"

"Ren." Roman stops my anxious rambling. "That perfectly reasonable question is not too personal. You've choked on my cock, and I had your pussy for breakfast. As far as I'm concerned, that means you can ask me anything."

"Oh," I say flatly, realizing my response was due to Lewis gaslighting me anytime I asked what I also thought were perfectly reasonable questions. Of course, I now know it wasn't my questions that were too personal. It was him trying to hide the fact that he's married.

"And the answer is no. I don't have any children." He rehangs the pewter carriage. "What about you?"

"No." I shake my head. "I don't really want kids."

"Me either," he says casually. "Though, I'm a little surprised you didn't ask if I had grandkids first."

"You'd be one fine grandpa." I laugh, then it occurs to me that despite all the teasing, I don't actually know. "How old are you?"

"Forty-seven, which makes me older than you by . . .?"

For an accountant, I'm really bad at doing math in my head. Luckily, I just turned thirty, making it easy. "Seventeen years."

"Well, for what it's worth . . ." He sighs dramatically and my stomach drops like a rock. "I think you'd make a damn fine grandma too."

I exhale my held breath and smack him in the chest, chuckling. "Bastard."

Once we have a basket full of mixed ornaments, we go to opposite sides of the store to look at the clothing. After a few minutes, Roman texts me.[2]

You mind coming to the dressing rooms? I want your opinion.

I head to the back of the store where the dressing room area is, a row of curtained stalls stretching to the left and right.

"Roman?"

"Over here," he calls out.

I walk down the side with his voice, waiting for him to pop his head out or something. Instead, my heart nearly jumps out of my chest when I'm suddenly grabbed through a curtain and strongly yanked into the stall. I

---

2. Stop playing "I Feel Love"—Freya Ridings

yell as loud as I can, but it's pointless when a palm clamps firmly over my mouth.

AND THEN COMES BAMBI

Roman

I t happens fast. I pull her deeper into the stall.[1] Her muffled screams vibrate on my palm as I sit on the bench inside, tugging her down on my lap. Before grabbing her, I already pulled down my pants and put a condom on.

"Shh, you're okay." I know the moment she recognizes my voice because she sags with relief, her back tightly held to my chest, my hard cock under her. "I'll remove my hand if you promise me one thing."

She nods, and I can feel her fast, deep exhales on my fingers

---

1. Play "Gimme Love"—Rosenfeld

I keep my voice low but no less authoritative. "You're gonna ride my cock and make me come without making a sound. Can you do that for me?" She nods faster.

"Good girl," I purr coarsely and slowly pull my hand away. As I do, she quickly rucks up the skirt of her dress. She's in the same outfit she wore to dinner with one noticeable difference.

"You're fucking perfect," I growl into her neck when I feel the heat of her bare pussy through the condom. "Put me inside you." The order comes out rushed and hungry. No matter how hard I try, I can't hide the effect she has on me. I should stop trying.

A whiny moan leaves her as she lowers herself onto my cock. "And remember, not a sound." My last word is strangled as I try to take my own advice while my cock slips into her slick cunt. "Fuck, you feel so good," I can't help but whisper roughly into her ear.

She has her legs on either side of mine, then begins slowly riding me. I feel her inner muscles squeeze every time she forces herself back down on my cock. My fingers grip her hips and sink into the soft flesh. Every wet slide of her pussy has me digging in my fingers just a little more.

"That's it, baby, fuck me just like that." Pleasure spreads through my body like molten lust. It burns and warms at the same time.

The harder she rides me, the more her heavy breaths morph into moans. Finally, she stutters out, "I-I don't think I c-can be quiet. Will you c-cover my mouth?"

As soon as I do, she releases a moan that would have been loud enough to get us caught if not for my palm, as if her pleasure could no longer be contained. Something I can quite viscerally relate to as my own feels like a dam about to break.

"Fuck, fu—" I bite down hard on her shoulder in a last-ditch effort to stay quiet. She screams into my hand as my teeth dig into the muscle. Something about her muffled cry sends me over the edge. It's desperate and raw. And the sweetest, most erotic soundtrack as I come, groaning into her shoulder.

"I've never been a huge fan of shopping, but you may have just changed my mind," I mutter teasingly as we walk to the cashier to check out.

Her cheeks are still flushed a pretty pink, and I bet her thighs are still slick. "Yeah, thrifting is great." She tries to sound cool and casual.

She's not going to get away with that, not with me.

I subtly reach for her ass and squeeze one of the supple cheeks, hard. Hard enough her whole back tenses. "This being a thrift store had nothing to do with it." She gives me a guilty little look. "And you know it."

"I might have some idea." She smiles mischievously and leans into my side. I can't resist wrapping my arm around her waist to keep her there.

At the register, the cashier scans our basket of ornaments one by one. I see Ren eyeing a flyer advertising the local ice rink's holiday special. Rather than continue to listen to the incessant beep , I ask her, flicking my chin at the flyer, "Do you have any plans for the rest of the day?"

"Nope. No plans." The smile she gives me makes my lungs stop working, like with one question I've made all her wildest dreams come true. What did I do to deserve someone as precious as her? "You?"

I tongue my cheek. "All free."

The Fox family has bookmaking operations for just about every professional team or sporting event in the city. The South Harbor Ice Arena, home to the June Harbor Hailstorms, is no different. So when the head of security spots Ren and me as we check out our rental skates, he immediately looks like he just got caught with his pants down.

I'm rarely involved at the street level. So, if I'm here, it usually means someone has *really* fucked up. He swallows and says something into his radio before making his way over to us with a grave face.

Ren, who's chatting with the rental guy, hasn't noticed our silent interaction or his approach. And I'd really prefer he doesn't look like he's about to shit his pants when she does.

I try to get ahead of it as soon as he says, "Roman, we weren't expecting you."

"I'm not here on business, Mike," I assure him, and he visibly relaxes, just in time for Ren to turn around. "Mike, this is Ren, and we're just here to skate."

"Well, we're happy to have you," he says overenthu-siastically. Ren smiles politely and says it's nice meeting him but gives me shifty eyes. "Today's on the house. Got that, Ryan?" He looks to the guy getting our skates.

"Yeah, sure," Ryan says like he could give two flying shits. "I'll still need them back ten minutes before close."

"That won't be a problem." I grab Ren's and my skates off the counter and lift them as if cheersing. "And thanks, Mike."

"Enjoy the ice." He sends us off.

"So . . . ," Ren begins curiously. "You come here a lot for business?"

"Not a lot," I say as she sits down on benches closer to the rink. I lower to one knee in front of her and pick up her foot.

"I gather this falls under the less than legal side of things?" she asks while I untie her boot. We stopped by her place on the way here so she could change into something that wouldn't cause frost bite in unmention-able places or get her arrested for public indecency if she fell.

I slip off her shoe and start loosening the laces on the skates. "Something like that."

"Got it," she smiles tersely.

I hate being evasive like this, but it's for her own good. Mostly.

Still, it grates something inside me.

"There are a lot of reasons I'm being vague, the greatest of which is for your safety. If that's ever not enough, we can talk about it, alright?" I try to be diplomatic but also sensible.

Cass hated that I couldn't tell her everything. She felt like I was always lying to her rather than strategically and purposefully withholding information that she didn't need to know.

"I get it." Ren nods, her tone lighter, more understanding. "Plausible deniability and all that."

"Something like that," I say again, but this time my lip quirks with a small smile.

I finish putting on and lacing up her skates, then quickly do mine. She watches me and asks, "Seems like you really know what you're doing?"

"I played a little hockey growing up," I admit. "But it's been a while since I've been on the ice, so no laughing if I look like Bambi out there."

She laughs. "Well, I've never skated before, so hopefully it's like riding a bike because if not, we'll both be on our asses."

"I'd hate for anything to hurt that perfect ass of yours," I tease as I help her to her feet. She wobbles a little on the rubber floor and stumbles a step closer to me to regain her balance, squeezing my hands.

I lean forward, and she naturally tilts her face up. Our noses almost brush. Then, right before I kiss her, I add, "Other than my hand of course."

I'm trying to coax her away from the boards that she is gripping onto for dear life. "I know it's counterintuitive, but you're more likely to fall if you keep holding that."

By the glare she shoots me, you'd think I just horrifically insulted the world's cutest puppies. "Says the man skating *backward* after saying it's been a while and not to laugh if he looks like Bambiiiii," she squeals as her legs slip out from under her and her arms windmill.

I grab her by the waist, catching her before she becomes Bambi herself. Once she's no longer flailing, I take both of her hands in mine. "Do you believe me now?"

She huffs, trying to blow a lock of hair out of her face that fell during the scuffle. "Begrudgingly."

I help her out, tucking a wayward strand behind her ear then slowly beginning to move, skating backward to gently pull her along with me. She never takes her untrusting stare off her feet, her movements choppy and awkward.

"Try not to overthink it. Your body will naturally figure out how to keep itself upright."

She squeezes my hands as she wobbles again. "How am I supposed to do that? It's *all* I can think about."

"Tell me something I don't know about you," I suggest.

"You're the first man to ever make me come—" *That* gets her attention off her feet. Her eyes are huge when she suddenly looks up as if shocked those words came out of her mouth. "Any chance I didn't say that out loud?"

"I was expecting something more along the lines of a broken arm when you were six, but . . ." I try not to laugh in the face of her clear mortification.

"Oh my god." She groans and squeezes her eyes shut then cracks one open. "Does that freak you out?"

"What?" Now I'm genuinely shocked. "*God, no.*"

She grimaces like she doesn't believe me.

"Not only do I find it incredibly hot that I'm the only man alive who knows what it feels like to make you tremble like a dirty, little slut . . ." Her eyes widen again at my word choice and I smirk, glad that they had the desired effect of successfully distracting her from her misplaced embarrassment. "But it makes me far less likely to murder your dipshit of an ex if I ever see him."

That gets her to throw her head back with a laugh, and I feel like I've won the fucking lottery.

"And do you realize you've now skated halfway around the rink?"

"Would you look at that." She looks around at our progress in delighted surprise. When her gaze returns to me, she says, "Okay, your turn. Tell me something I don't know about you."

I don't even have to think about it. "I didn't drink coffee regularly until three months ago."

She smiles and nods knowingly. "Is that when you first had June Bug's? I swear it's the best in the city."

"No. That's when I first saw you."

JUST KEEP READING

Roman

Her face goes blank, and my heart skips a beat. Then, the most endearing, genuine smile slowly spreads across it, and I feel like I could fly, or at the very least spin around with her above my head like an Olympic figure skater.

"Does that freak *you* out?" I turn the question back on her.

She laughs as if it's an absurd thing to ask. With apparently newfound confidence on skates, she flings her arms around my neck and pulls herself to my chest.

"As long as it doesn't freak *you* out that every morning I'd secretly wish you'd be there," she confides, giving me smile so big my cheeks hurt.

Her blue eyes dazzle up at me under the bright lights of the arena, and I never want to lose this very view. "So, after these five days—"

"*Oh my god*, I know him!" Ren gasps, pointing at a TV hanging above the eating area by concessions.

I can't believe I was so close to saying something so reckless, so selfish. Thank God I don't think Ren caught a word I said. I watch the TV, feeling like I just dodged a bullet.

On the news, a sixty-something-year-old white man walks down the courthouse steps to a mass of reporters' microphones and cameras. The ticker at the bottom reads, "Cult Leader Indicted for Fraud along with Several Big Oil Executives."

"This is crazy," Ren says for the third time on our drive back home—well, my place. She's been devouring articles on her phone about Johnathon Willis, the "Divine Elder" she saw on the news. "Apparently, these oil companies had been *intentionally* contaminating our water and soil to conduct studies on toxicity and exposure to different chemicals and such. Because we were so insular, our community was the perfect control group."

"That's inhumane," I say, disgusted.

"It's awful!" she agrees. "And these companies are supposed to get signed waivers and consent from everyone taking part in their experiments. But instead of telling any of us, Willis forged all the forms and pocketed all the compensation we were supposed to get for *literally being poisoned.*"

She goes silent for a moment, then, for the second time in an hour, gasps loudly in utter shock. "*Oh my god.* I got an interview."

I don't know why my chest sinks at the news, especially when she's clearly elated. "I thought you were taking time off for a little bit?" I selfishly hope whatever the new job is, it doesn't start before Christmas.

"I am. This is for a volunteer position at a gorilla sanctuary. I thought I could fulfill little Ren's dream until I find something paying for big Ren." She laughs.

"That's great." I reach over to place my hand on her thigh. "I'm really happy for you. When's the interview?"

"Tomorrow at one." She sounds a little nervous. "They wanted to squeeze it in before their office closes for the holidays. Which, I think, is a good sign, right?

Like, even if they aren't eager to interview me specifically, they must be trying to fill the position quickly."

"I'm sure it has to do with you being the applicant. Do you want me to drop you off at your place so you can be ready for tomorrow?" I try to keep my tone neutral even though I'd be crossing all my fingers and toes if I could.

"It's after lunch so I figured I could still spend the night." It makes me pleased and, for some reason, a little proud that she assumed she would be sleeping over again. I must not show it on my face because she starts, "I mean, if that's cool with you, or I could go home. I don't know what you had in mind—"

"What I had in mind"—I stop her spiral in its tracks—"is taking advantage of your tree-decorating expertise, then taking advantage of you in bed—" I tilt my head side to side as if indecisive. "Or in the kitchen or on the couch, hell, even the hallway floor. I'm not that picky. Then waking up to a repeat of this morning."

I finish just as we pull up to a red light, so I can look over and see her perfect, closed-mouth smile that's a combination of bashful and giddy.

She picks my hand off her leg and presses a kiss to my palm. "I very much like the sound of that."

Ren

The overhead lights are off in Roman's living room, and he's seconds away from plugging in the ones on the Christmas tree when I realize, "We forgot the star!"

I switch back on the room's lights and immediately start digging through the bag from the thrift store. After tossing all the extra paper used to protect the ornaments, I find our star buried at the bottom. It looks like something someone DIYed, tubes of cardboard formed into points then slathered with Mod Podge and doilies.

Roman crouches down in front of me. "Get on my shoulders."

"*What?*"

"Unless you have another idea for reaching the top of the tree." He makes a very good point.

Hesitantly, I clutch the star to my chest then lift one leg over his shoulder. Once I'm fully seated, he folds his arms over my shins and asks, "Ready?"

"Yep," I say, surprised with how sturdy I feel—I think there's a metaphor somewhere in there, but any deeper meaning is lost on me once he starts standing. I wobble back, but his arms are like bars across my legs and I easily right myself.

He takes a step closer to the tree. I love the smell of the fresh pine. The star fits perfectly over the top sprig.

"Done!" I proudly proclaim, and he lowers back down.

Once I'm back on my own two feet, he looks at me. "Lights?"

"*Yes,*" I say excitedly. I go to turn off the lights, and he goes to plug in the tree. I remind him one last time, "Don't forget to close your eyes!"

"One, two, *three,*" he counts down. I squeeze my eyes shut and flip the switch while he closes his and plugs the cord into the outlet.

I start blindly shuffling toward the tree and hear him doing the same.

"No peeking," he warns unnecessarily.

"Please." I wave my arms in front of me. "I take this *very* seriously."

My hand hits something hard but squishy, and Roman chuckles. "I knew you were an ass girl."

He must turn around while I'm laughing because the next thing I feel is both of his hands grabbing mine. He pulls me to him, then wraps his arms around my shoulders, hugging my back to his chest. His chin rests on top of my head, and I think this singular moment is the happiest I've been in a really long time. I almost don't want to open my eyes, fearing that it all might actually be a dream.

On the count of three again, we open our eyes together and . . .

"That is a couch," Roman states.

I laugh, realizing we're turned around, and he spins us to face the tree.

And there it is in all its glory. A string of rainbow lights woven between the limbs and the sad, plain ornaments that were once all alone, now with plenty of friends.

He hums approvingly. "Well done, Miss Calloway. Well done."

Later that night, I'm reading one of Roman's books in Roman's bed, wearing Roman's giant tee shirt.[1] It feels like a scene stolen from the future. One of an unremarkable couple doing unremarkable things but being remarkably happy.

Despite the short time we've known each other and the unconventional way we met, I feel safe, comfortable, and completely at ease.

And I think that's all I ever really wanted. If I were being the good girl, I just wanted someone to be good to me in return. Somehow, that was always too much to ask for. Roman has shown me it's not.

He comes out of the bathroom, a white towel just barely able to wrap around his waist. A few rogue drops of water from his shower remain, cutting down his chiseled chest and abs. He looks down at the book in my hand. "I hope you don't mind I started this?"

"Not at all," he says with a distant tone that makes me wonder if he even heard me. His eyes trace my bent legs

---

1. Play "Lights On"—H.E.R.

where I sit on top of the covers. My heart beats a little faster, like it does anytime his attention zeros in on me.

He steps up to the side of the bed. I'm about to put the book down when he says in that gravelly tone that makes my pussy clench, "Don't stop."

He grabs my ankles, then spins my legs over the side of the bed. I hold tightly onto the book as he flips me onto my stomach next.

"Keep reading," he orders, and I hear his towel drop.

He tugs my hips to the edge of the mattress, my toes grazing the floor. My body hums with anticipation, my bare pussy put on display when he pushes the shirt up my back. My chest pounds. His hard cock slides against my ass as he rocks slowly back and forth, in no rush to get a condom. Earlier this evening, Dr. Romero called us both separately to inform us our tests came back clean.

"Tell me again why you didn't want to postpone the doc's visit," he says in such a deep, hungry tone, it's almost a growl.

"Next time you use me like your own personal fuck-doll, I don't want anything in between us." My words come out feathered and quiet even though saying them exhilarates me.

"Mm-hmm." He groans. "Now, keep reading while I use this tight little cunt for my own pleasure."

I gasp loudly when he gives me no other warning before slamming inside me. "*God—*" I quickly bite my tongue and force myself to focus on the book in front of me. I start a sentence I have no hope of finishing as he withdraws part way, then pounds back in.

His hands on my hips pull me back on his every thrust. "Fuck, baby, you really are so goddamn tight like this." He's right. I'm just wet enough that it doesn't hurt, but just barely.

"*Mm-hmm,*" I whimper.

"You're hugging my cock so perfectly, so fucking good for me, aren't you, sweet girl?" he croons, slowing his thrusts to hard, sensual rolls of his pelvis.

"*Yes . . . please.*" I don't even know what I'm pleading for. All I know is that I want to be a good girl for him.

"Please what? Please stretch your tight little pussy?"

"Yes, yes," I mewl.

"Please use you like a good little whore?" He picks back up his pace, shoving me against the bed with every punch of his hips. "Please fuck you until I get what I want then leave you desperate and dripping for more?"

His voice gets rougher with every question, like the more he taunts me, the more he's torturing himself.

"Or maybe I want to leave you a trembling mess, make you come again and again for me." Every word, every stroke, every finger digging into my hip claws at my inhibition, at any preconceived ideas about what I *should* want or enjoy. And as they shred, I'm left only with my desire, every wonderful, wanton spark of it.

"Yes. Please. All of it," I beg. He reaches over me and plucks the book from my hand.

In my periphery, I catch him using the dust jacket flap as a bookmark before setting it on the nightstand. He pulls out completely, then grabs me by the waist before tossing me farther onto the bed. I lie flat on my stomach now, only my feet dangling off the side.

"Stay just like that," he demands.

The bed rocks as he climbs onto it. He kneels, straddling my thighs. His palms knead my ass, then move up and down my back. "You're so beautiful like this, all laid out for me. I could spend all night tasting every inch of you." I moan in pleasure as he massages my shoulders then sits back up. "But that won't be tonight. So right now, I need you to lift your hips for me, beautiful."

I draw my hips up. "That's my girl." He groans as he slips into my now soaking pussy. With his hands planted by my sides, he forces my pelvis back down with his.

When he thrusts, the weight of him on top of me expels all the air in my lungs with a moan.

His hips pin me down so tightly that each time he pounds into me from behind, my clit rubs against the bed. It's rough and deep and *still* not enough. Every spike of pleasure is followed by the hope that the next one will be stronger, harder.

"Fuck me into the mattress. Fuck me into the matt—" I stutter.

He delivers, pinning both my hands behind my back.

Soon, I can't catch my breath, my pussy is throbbing, and my clit is pulsing. All I can do is bite the sheets and take it.

"Is this what you wanted? For me to wreck your greedy fucking pussy?" he rasps hoarsely.

I nod deliriously. "*So—good—*" I try to speak between each forced exhale. My head swims. Desire and pressure is all I can focus on, the building tension, my muscles constricting for a release. "I'm going to—about to com—fuck, fuck, *Roman*, please."

He releases my hands and flattens his chest and stomach to my back, wrapping one arm across my chest. His breath is hot against my neck. My body clenches under him, my needy whines incoherent.

He keeps his thrusts heavy and hard as he whispers roughly in my ear, "That's it. Come all over my cock like my good fucking slut." And I *shatter*.

I shatter like a fucking supernova, hot and bright.

"*Fuck, fuuckk,*" he growls, my pussy milking his cock as he comes, hard and hot, his body enveloping mine.

His supporting arm shakes as he tries to catch his breath, panting into the nook of my neck. His weight and heat are the most comforting things and exactly what I need right now. Maybe all I ever needed.

It feels wholly inadequate, but I say it anyway, breathless and blissful. "*Thank you.*"

19

THICC

Roman

R en left earlier this morning to go home before her interview. Since then, I've changed the sheets on both beds, done two loads of laundry, gone to the gym, cleaned my already clean kitchen, vacuumed the pine needles that had fallen off the Christmas tree, and gotten my car washed.

Now that I've exhausted every possible distraction, I'm left sitting on my couch, staring at my phone on the coffee table as if the harder I focus on it, the sooner it will ring.

I promised myself I would wait for Ren to text me first after her interview. A promise I already broke once to wish her good luck, even though I'm sure she doesn't need it. The desire to be near her consumes me. And scares me.

Because what happens when these five days end?[1] A desire like this doesn't come with an expiration date.

I knew the first night I met her that I'd break all my rules for her. But does she even want me to?

There's a reason I've avoided dating since Cass left. My job—my *life*—is dangerous, turbulent, and unpredictable. Under the best of circumstances, it would be selfish to pull anyone into my world.

And Ren's circumstances are far from ideal. She recently got out of a terrible relationship with the world's biggest idiot, got fired for no good reason, and just found out that she grew up as an unknowing participant in a sick experiment.

She shouldn't have to go through all that alone . . . . No, no, I'm just trying to justify wanting her for Christmas, and New Year's, and every day after that.

And who am I to think I could support her? She doesn't need someone who sneaks out in the middle of the night to take care of business that he'll never share.

---

1. Play "Venus"—Mackenzy Mackay as indicated

Right now, I can't imagine not putting her first, but I'm sure it will happen. It's what I do, who I am.

I fucked up the moment I agreed to her proposal.

My phone lights up with a notification, and I practically leap off the couch to grab it.

Ren: I'm gonna go for a run to burn off these post-interview jitters then jumping in the shower, but after that I'm free.

I read her text and realize accepting her proposal wasn't the moment I fucked up.

Roman: Leave your door unlocked.

I fucked up the moment I thought I could walk away after only five days.[2]

My heart thumps as I place my hand on Ren's front door handle. I don't know why, but a part of me half-expected to find it locked. So, when it seamlessly turns and I open the door a crack, my anticipation is laced with relief.

Stepping inside her townhouse, I understand her offense at my undecorated tree. A mirror in the foyer is

---

2. Pause "Venus"—Mackenzy Mackay

wrapped in fresh garland, instantly greeting me with its classic holiday scent of pine needles and happy memories.

Like the front windows of June Bug, she's hand painted a little snowscape on the glass. Snowflakes fall from the top of the mirror onto the charming winter scene at the bottom. On one side, a man drags a freshly cut Christmas tree behind him, while two kids in a sled fly down a hill on the other. In between them stands a little family of snowmen. Even though my childhood, growing up in New Orleans, couldn't be further from the scene she's depicted, there's something nostalgic about it. I always went to bed Christmas Eve praying for a white Christmas.

I wonder what Christmas on a corrupt hippie commune is like and make a note to ask her. After our shower, of course.

The entrance opens up to the living room, where the couch is draped with a green and red plaid blanket and all the pillows are holiday themed with embroidered reindeer or jolly holiday phrases. From here, I can look straight back to her kitchen. There's a Santa-shaped cookie jar on the counter and back doors framed with fronds of holly.

Then, of course, there is her tree, an absolute spectacle with not only ornaments, but ribbons and tinsel too. And instead of average string lights, there's probably two dozen little candleholders clipped to the branches with electric candles. Beautifully wrapped boxes already sit underneath. It looks like the same person wrapped them all, and there are no tags or cards I can see. Are they gifts or simply more decorations?

The idea that the boxes could be empty when her heart is so full makes mine hurt.

I follow the sound of running water and off-key singing up a flight of stairs and down a hall.[3] As I draw closer, I'm struck with the domesticity of it all as I imagine coming home to this very soundtrack. Knowing it won't be, I don't expect the following pang in my chest, hollow and aching. I do my best to ignore it when I find, what I assume, is her bedroom.

It is somehow exactly how I pictured it, a mix of messy and tidy. The laundry basket is overflowing onto the floor, but her bed is made neatly with several throw pillows. Instead of curtains, the canopy bed frame is wrapped in more Christmas lights.

---

3. Continue playing "Venus"—Mackenzy Mackay until end of chapter

The door to the en suite is ajar. I can hear Ren and smell floral soap on the steam, but I can't see her yet. My cock is already growing at the mental images alone, water sluicing down the perfect slopes of her body.

I strip as quietly as possible, my pulse quickening. I lightly push the door all the way open and bite back a groan. Steam has fogged the shower glass some, but not nearly enough to obscure my view. Any mental images can't hold a fucking candle to the real thing.

She turns toward me, and her singing is cut off with a startled sound. She must not have heard me, but in less than a second, her surprise morphs into a welcoming smile.

"Hi," she says in that same bashful yet excited way she did when we ran into each other at the Den.

I step into the shower. "Hi."

She moves out from under the stream and wrings out her long hair in a twist. "I was just about to get out," she admits with a slight bite of her lip.

"No, you're not. You're staying right here." I grab her rope of twisted hair and pull her to me. Her mouth falls open at the sudden tug as I crush our bodies together under the running water.

Her face, ruddy from working out, and her lashes, darkened by water, make her eyes look an even more vibrant blue . . . *just beautiful.* Her palms move up and down my chest and she gives me a look that says *is that so?*

A smile flits across her face as I bend down to kiss her. It's a light one that I drag out, savoring the soft warmth of her lips. She melts into me as I wrap my arm around her lower back and let go of her hair to cup the nape of her neck.

When I finally pull away, her eyes flutter open, making a drop fall from her lashes, and she sways a little as if left unsteady by my kiss. It's such a small movement, but it hits me like a wave.

In the corner of the shower, there is a small step stool with bottles. I move the shampoo to the shower floor and pick up the conditioner and stool. I set the stool back down toward the middle of the shower, then pop the lid of the conditioner.

Ren watches me with heavy breaths and hooded eyes. The way she looks at me makes me feel like a king. I drizzle a small amount of conditioner onto my cock, and her brows pinch slightly, like she's unsure of where this is going.

"I haven't been able to stop thinking about fucking your thick thighs since I got your text."

The small crease between her eyes relaxes, but she still asks softly, already a little breathless, "How?"

"Step up here, beautiful. Back to me." I nod to the stool. It doesn't budge on the stone floor as she stands on top of it. *Good.* "Hands on the wall."

She doesn't have to bend over much to place both palms on the tiled walls. I use one hand to spread the conditioner over my cock while dragging my other hand down the beautiful slope of her slightly arched back.

The water beats down on us both from the side. I nearly close the distance between us. Her breath catches when the head of my cock just kisses the place her two thighs meet. My own lungs lock up as I grab her hips with both hands and nudge my dick deeper.

"Move your feet closer together," I order in a deep, rugged tone. She presses her legs together, hugging my cock with her hot, wet thighs, and I groan. "That's it. Perfect. That's fucking *perfect*."

My grip on her hips tightens as I take an experimental rock backward then forward, making sure that the stool remains steady. She's now a little more than half a foot off the ground, making her just the right height.

"*Fuck* . . ." My length glides smoothly between her thighs.

I repeat the movement again, a bit stronger, and she moans softly. Again a little harder, and her fingers flatten against the tile. I thrust in and out. As I increase speed and force, her soft mewls get louder and louder.

"God, you just love being used, don't you?"

"*Yes,*" she responds so needily that I can't help but grip her pillowy flesh harder and fuck her thighs with heavy punches of my hips, making her rock forward again and again. The sweet sounds she makes every time my cock drags across the front of her pussy are fucking addicting.

Chasing them turns my grip bruising, my fingertips digging into her soft skin. I don't even realize it until she exhales quietly. "*Ow* . . ."

"Shit, I'm sorry," I say, immediately pulling back and lightening my hold.

"No, no," she says almost desperately. "Don't stop. I want it. Please, Roman, don't be scared of breaking me."

And fuck, do I want to break her. I want to obliterate the memory of any other man's touch. I want to ink my fingerprints into her beautiful curves. And when I make her shatter, I want to be the only one who catches her pieces.

But she isn't mine to break and put back together for safekeeping. She's only mine for three more days. I have to be careful. "Okay, but I want your word. Gimme your word so I'll know when to stop."

"Giraffe." Even though I can't see her face, I know she's smiling.

That makes the corner of my mouth turn up as I murmur, "Good girl." Then I slap her ass and wrap her hair around my fist before continuing to use her like my perfect little fuckdoll.

Ren

The sound of our wet bodies slapping together fills the shower. My scalp stings from the tight leash he's made with my hair. Every thrust comes with a sharp tug, making my back bow.

"Fuck yeah, arch your back just like that, baby. Show me how much you want me to fuck your sweet thighs."

I mewl at the next thrust because the more I arch, the more of my pussy he drags against. My clit is aching for direct stimulation, but this tease of him gliding in and out of my lips is equally delicious.

I squeeze my thighs tighter together, reveling in the feel of his thick cock pushing back and forth, the conditioner still providing a smooth slide. My whole body is buzzing.

"Fuck, fuck," he growls under his breath before ripping me away from the wall and kicking the stool out of the way. He spins me around, roughly spewing, "On your knees, on your fucking knees."

I fall to the floor, feeling like the wind has been knocked out of me, but it's just the sight of him, muscles rippling, water dripping, eyes burning.

He looms above me like a god.

His voice is strained as he strokes his cock in his fist. "I gonna come all over your perfect tits. I want you fucking *painted* with my cum."

His jaw clenches tightly and his abs go rigid, his breath ragged and torn. His eyes close right before he comes, but only for a second. He seems to force them open so he can watch his hot cum spill across my chest.

He doesn't stare at his work long though, instead pulling me to my feet and saying, hushed and husky, "Fuck, *come here.*"

His mouth crashes to mine, and I unconsciously rub my thighs together. I'm not surprised to feel that they are slick with more than just conditioner. "God, that was so fucking hot. I'm dripping." I moan against his lips, then, feeling emboldened, tease, "You should feel how wet I am."

He chuckles softly then gives my bottom lip a little tug with his teeth. "I'd rather taste it."

Giving my hips a gentle shove, he encourages me back toward the built-in shower bench. I sit, and the hungry look he gives me instinctively has me spreading my knees and planting my feet on the edge of the bench.

"That's my girl." He nods approvingly, a proud tilt to his lips.

Before kneeling in front of me, he grabs a washcloth off a hook. His beautiful brown eyes look up at me adoringly, making it harder to breathe as he tenderly wipes the conditioner off my inner thighs.

When he's done, he keeps his heavy gaze on me as he drags his tongue over the same spot. His beard is a rough but welcome sensation mixed with heat of the shower and flush of my skin. He kisses the stretch marks at the peak of my thigh, his eyelids fluttering like it's the sweetest thing he's ever tasted.

I don't know how I'm going to let this go in a few days, let *him* go.

Something must show on my face because when he opens his eyes, he asks, "You okay?"

"Yes, yes," I say assuredly, then add sassily, "Just ready for you to stop torturing me."

He laughs then grabs my ass, hooking my thighs with his arms and tugging me to the very edge.

"Lean back, baby." He puts a wide palm on my stomach as I recline onto my hands.

"I like when you call me baby."

"Yeah?" His eyes soften like just maybe he likes calling me that too.

"Yeah, it makes me feel like . . . I don't know, a cinnamon roll or something." I giggle.

"All dripping and sweet, huh?" he jokes, then nips my thigh before dragging his nose up my slit.

He kisses me right above my pussy, a devilish glint to his heated gaze. "And what about when I call you a little slut or whore?"

"I like that too," I answer softly, feeling shy all of a sudden. My stomach flutters, butterflies beating under his palm. *Can he feel them?* "But can I still be a good girl?"

"Of course." A loose smile spreads on his lips right before he flattens his tongue for a lascivious drag through my pussy. "'Cause you're mine, *my* good little whore." Then, as if that concludes the discussion, he covers my clit with his mouth.

"Oh, fuck," I gasp as he laves my clit with wide, heavy strokes of his tongue.

His movements are slow, intentional, like he truly just wants me to feel every little sensation. His palm presses down on my lower stomach so I can watch every tantalizing move he makes.

He slips two fingers into me and groans. "God, you're fucking soaked. Just from me fucking your pretty thighs? Or was it me painting you like my cum slut?"

"Every—" My sharp moan cuts me off as he returns to licking my pussy. "*Thing,*" I cry next, his fingers curling inside me. And I don't just mean right now. I mean all the time, every little thing he does feels like a gift just for me.

From the first night when he covered the scratchy hay with his jacket, he continues to show me that my wants and needs aren't superfluous, that my comfort isn't an inconvenience. The realization overwhelms me with emotion. My hands on either side of his head tilt his face toward me. I feel desperate, almost frantic as I beg, "Kiss me. Will you kiss me? Can you—"

His lips are on mine before I can finish. I taste myself on his tongue. His fingers knit into my hair, and while he's still kneeling, I wrap my legs around his waist. My hands glide down his strong back, water pouring onto it.

I've wrapped myself around him, but it still doesn't feel like enough to calm this harried desire. I pull away, gasping for air and begging, "I need you to fuck me, please. I need—"

"Shh, I'm here, sweet girl." His voice is like cool silk against my heated skin and the way I'm burning up inside. "I'll take care of you."

He partially stands and wraps his arms under me. He pulls me onto his cock, slipping me off the bench before standing all the way up. I'm so relieved and I don't know why.

Why did I feel like all of a sudden, I couldn't breathe until he was inside me? Why, as he carries me to my bed, leaving a trail of water, does it feel like I could cry?

I'm hardly aware of the mattress and fluffy comforter under me. All I know is his body above mine, hard and hot and still dripping wet, and the way he rocks into me while holding me while softly murmuring, "*That's my good girl.*"

As my heels dig into his ass, he fucks me hard but sweet, and I'm aware of nothing but the growing sensation of weightlessness as I lose myself to him and *everything* he is.

HAPPY ENDINGS

Ren

E arlier this week, I felt like I was living in a movie, stuffing a stupid cardboard box with fake plants, wondering how it could possibly have a happy ending.

Now, I still feel like I'm in a movie, but one where the "flames" of my fake candles flicker in the background while Roman absentmindedly picks up my feet resting in his lap. He starts rubbing his thumb into the balls of my feet as the second one in our *The Office* Christmas episodes marathon begins. Though, I spend more time watching him than the TV, wondering if this, too, will have a happy ending.

Occasionally, he looks over at me, and I make a poor attempt to hide my smile and pretend I wasn't staring.

He smirks as his gaze returns to the TV and mine to him—I know all the episodes by heart anyway.

His phone rings, and he excuses himself as he lifts my feet and stands up. "I'm sorry. I have to get this."

"Cash," he answers, walking to the kitchen. Even at this distance, I can hear someone or something loud on the call. It sounds chaotic. His jaw clenches and his face turns stoic and stony. I feel a chill in the air as he flatly replies, "Stay safe. I'll be right there."

Shoving his phone back in his pocket, he looks at me, a flit of sorrow in his eyes before his expression hardens to that of a soldier.

"I have to go." He doesn't offer an apology or explanation, even though something tells me he wants to. His eyes dart to the now empty spot on the couch next to me with a flash of longing and my throat tightens.

I get up, and he shakes his hand. "You don't have to."

"I want to," I say unequivocally and meet him at my front door.

I don't ask if everything is okay. It's clearly not, and I get the distinct feeling this is one of the situations he can't tell me about.

My chest hammers. I'm scared. Not for myself, but for him and whatever he is walking into.

"Roman," I say, his hand on the doorknob, and his throat bobs on a heavy swallow. He meets my gaze and my breath feels shallow. I take a front door key off the foyer table and place it into his other palm, wrapping his fingers around it and holding his hand with mine. "I know we're not going to bed together, but if you need me . . ." I kiss his folded knuckles. "You can have me."

The ghost of a smile passes over his lips before he presses them to my forehead. "See you soon, sweet girl."

As the door closes behind him, I find myself wondering again, will this movie have a happy ending?

Roman

The wind off the bay is bitter cold as I wait with Roan, the second youngest Fox brother, for the cleaners to show up. The moon is still high in the sky outside the warehouse, but I'm sure the sun will be rising by the time they finish. They've got one hell of a mess to clean up.

An unknown crew tried to rip off one of our recent shipments and met a bloody end. Unfortunately, I didn't get here before they took out one of ours with them, Connor. Cash is off notifying Dana, his wife, while Finn and Lochlan, the other two Foxes, are already chasing down leads to get to the person behind the hit.[1]

It doesn't matter that I got here as soon as I could or that I sent a two of the assailants to meet their maker when I did. As head of security for the syndicate, every loss still feels like a personal failure.

My mind can't stop picturing Ren asleep in her bed alone. Was our soldier's wife asleep when Cash knocked on her door? Will Ren be when I'm the one that doesn't return home one day? Because even though our five days are quickly coming to an end, I can't seem to imagine a future without her in it.

I spent three years with Cass and never once wondered where she'd be or what she'd be doing if Cash came knocking. Which is probably why I wasn't surprised the day I came home to an empty bed and handwritten note.

---

1. Play "Dusk Till Dawn (feat. Sia)"—ZAYN, Sia until end of chapter

There were plenty of nights like this one when I was with her, and never once did my skin feel too tight like it does now with the urge, the need, to get back to Ren.

"Is Reggie still away?" I ask Roan about his wife, who is visiting family in Mexico.

He takes a drag of his cigarette. "Yeah, but she'll be back for Christmas." Exhaling, he gives me a look from the corner of his eye. He chuckles dryly. "You can go."

"What?" I'm not used to being this transparent. First Cash, now Roan. It's like Ren's pulled back every protective layer.

He gives me a knowing smirk. "Go home, Roman. You have someone waiting for you. I don't."

I usually like to be the last one to leave scenes like this, but tonight, he doesn't need to tell me twice.

This time when I climb the stairs, there is no sound of running water, just the quiet sounds outside of a sleeping city. When I reach her room, she's asleep on her side, the covers tucked tightly under her chin. Her profile is sweet—practically angelic—against her pillow, her blonde hair piled in a loose knot on top of her head.

I slowly undress, watching her full lips part as she sighs in her sleep. I stand naked at the foot of her bed and realize that if I climb in beside her, if I let myself find comfort in her, I won't ever be able to go back.

I walk to the side of the bed and do it anyway.

She doesn't stir as I pull back the sheets and slide under them. As I inch closer, I catch the smell of her conditioner. The scent takes me right back to the shower and the feel of her wet body, so warm and supple. My cock swells at the memory.

The mattress creaks as I tuck in behind her, but she still doesn't stir. My heart races with an illicit sort of anticipation. I've never done this before, never pulled back the hem of a woman's pajama shorts while my cock leaked, hoping she doesn't wake up. It's somehow both wicked and sweet.

My fingers slip between her thighs first and part her lips, holding my breath so that I can hear any minuscule sign of her waking. I swallow the immediate groan that forms at the feel of her slickness. Even asleep, she's still wet for me.

I angle my hips closer, then guide my dick to her entrance, grinding my teeth tight together as my tip sinks into her velvet heat. My hand wraps around her front to slide up her soft stomach under her tank top as I slowly fill her. As I curve my body around hers and fully seat myself inside her wet and waiting cunt, she moans softly. Soft enough that I'm not sure if she's woken or still asleep.

I take a testing rock backward before slowly thrusting deeper. Her pussy clenches around me as if just noticing the intrusion and this time when she moans quietly, she pushes back against me.

"*Mmm,*" she hums sleepily and covers my hand below her sternum with her own. "You're home."

Home.

Was that what I was looking for when I felt the chill of the coastal breeze, when I climbed the steps, when I crawled in beside her? Was it not simply comfort I came seeking, but the comfort of home?

She guides my hand higher to cup her breast.

"Yeah, baby," I whisper, pumping in and out with shallow strokes so she stays flush against me. I kiss up the side of her neck. "I'm home."

WAKE-UP CALL

Ren

I don't know what time it was when Roman came home, but when we fell back asleep, the sun's first rays were painting the sky. So, when my phone starts ringing, all I know is the sky outside my window is a brilliant blue, the sun full and bright.

The first call I send to voicemail with a blind slap to the nightstand, snuggling closer to Roman, who, between when I fell back asleep and now, has put on a durag. The second time, it rings I begrudgingly roll over and actually look. My stomach drops when I see an unknown number. Eight out of ten odds it's my mom, and she'd only be calling this early if something was wrong.

"Mom?" I answer groggily.[1]

"Oh, good, you're alive." My blood goes cold.

I sit up, clutching the comforter to my chest. "*Lewis?*"

Roman, who up until this moment, I thought was still asleep, suddenly rolls over, alert.

"You had me worried, Serenity." For a split second, I feel bad, almost fooled by the drip of sincerity in his voice. "You haven't returned a single call or text. The least you could do is let me know you're okay—"

"Because I blocked you," I say firmly. Roman props himself up on his elbow and watches attentively, supportively.

"You *what?*" And just like that, any hint of genuine concern is gone. "How immature, Ren." I grind my teeth together and exhale tediously though my nose, waiting for his tantrum to end. "And to believe I was actually *concerned* about you, and all the while you were just acting like a goddamn child."

"Are you done?" I'm surprised my voice doesn't shake with rage. Which probably has something to do with Roman scooting closer, his hand slithering across the top of my thigh.

---

1. Play "S.L.U.T."—Bea Miller until end of chapter

"That's it?" he scoffs. "That's all you have to say to me?"

Roman's hand dips between my legs, his eyes full of devilish intent, and I bite back a giggle to say, "Well, now that you know I'm doing just fine, goodbye, Lewis. And don't bother calling me again. I'll be blocking this number too."

"Go ahead, it won't last long. You'll come crawling back. I was the best thing that ever happened to you . . ." I don't listen to the rest of his tirade, pulling the phone away from my ear.

"Don't hang up." Roman takes it from me before I can. Instead, he puts the call on speaker and reaches over me to set it on the bedside table. "Let him hear how well you're doing without him."

I slide out of my sitting position as he climbs on top of me. My blood thrums as he pushes my tits together before salaciously tracing each nipple with an exaggerated circle of his tongue. He groans softly as they instantly harden, turning a deeper rosy shade.

Lewis's prattling might as well be white noise for as much attention as I'm paying it. I only tune back in when Roman stops and gives a pointed look and nod toward the phone.

"Ren. Ren? Are you still there? Are you even listening to me?" His frustration makes me fill with glee.

Especially because as he's huffing and puffing, Roman is nudging my knees apart with his wide shoulders and settling between my legs. He drags his nose up the crease between my pussy and thigh, his soft breath and beard tickling the sensitive skin.

"*Yes,*" I exhale heavily. Lewis thinks I'm answering him, but really it's Roman making the first drag of his tongue through my slit.

"Good. Because I'm serious, Ren."

Serious about what? I never find out, too busy clamping my hand over my mouth as Roman sucks and swirls my clit with a heavy tongue. I release a muffled whimper when he stops, smirking up at me and pulling my hand away.

"Let him hear you," he whispers smugly.

"What? Is someone there?" I stifle a laugh at Lewis's confusion.

I can't deny the brazen thrill I get when I let the next moan slip out uninhibited.

"Huh? I can't hear you—"

"Oh, *yes*." I gasp as two thick fingers are thrust inside my dripping cunt. I grind my hips up, both hearing and feeling Roman's appreciative, rumbly groan in response.

"Ren, I can't hear you," Lewis snipes, growing increasingly irritated.

"God, yes." I mewl, digging my fingers into Roman's strong back and shoulders.

"Yes, *what*?" Lewis shouts, and I smile giddily, as much at Lewis's vexation as Roman's talented tongue.

He works me higher and higher, his fingers pumping in and out, and I rock harder and harder into him, chasing that exquisite rise of pressure and pleasure.

"Fuck, don't stop, don't stop," I bite out sharply, my toes curling into the sheets. I'm distantly aware of Lewis's irate cursing as he finally puts two and two together, but I'm too far gone to care.

In fact, his presence only makes me beg harder. "Oh fuck, Roman, I want you inside me. Please let me come on your cock."

I'll never know how Lewis responds because before filling me to the hilt, Roman slaps my phone away, making it fly off the table. I watch it skitter across the floor with wide eyes.

"If it's broken, I'll buy you a new one." Roman pants as he cages my head with his forearms and thrusts into me.

"You think I give a shit about my phone right now?" I laugh, and I think his deep, husky laugh in return is just about my favorite sound in the world.

Fifteen minutes later, a thunderstorm of knocks raps on my front door, simultaneous with one long, continuous buzz of my doorbell. Nestled closely on Roman's chest, the barrage of noise doesn't startle me. Instead, I'm more annoyed, if anything, as I instinctively reach for my phone to check the doorbell camera.

"Oops," I mutter with a small giggle as I come up empty-handed. My phone, of course, is still somewhere—potentially shattered—on my bedroom floor.

"I'll look," Roman offers with a crooked smile and slides out of bed to peer out the window down at my front stoop. He chuckles smugly. "This should be fun."

There's a confident, almost eager air about him as he pulls on his pants.

"Who is it?" I ask even though I knew the second his demeanor changed who it was.

Running his hand up my leg under the covers, he gives me a brief kiss and squeezes my knee. "Nothing for you to worry about."

He doesn't say it dismissively, and I have no doubt he can handle Lewis, yet I still get up. Throwing on my shorts and cami set, I insist, "Let me talk to him."

He nods, giving me a proud once-over, wetting his bottom lip. "Of course."

Even in pajamas, I've never felt more empowered than I do walking down the stairs with Roman behind me. Lewis doesn't stop his incessant knocking the entire time it takes us to reach the front door, but it doesn't bother me. In fact, I'm unashamed of the joy I take in knowing he's only getting more and more riled up while I have never felt calmer and more in control.

I open the door, and he sputters, all red and flustered, "Oh, oh, so this is who you've been cheating on me with?" He throws a hand in Roman's direction, standing at my back.

My jaw literally drops. I'm absolutely stunned. "*In what conceivable world are we still together?*" Flabbergasted, that's what I am.

"We never broke—"

I swiftly cut off whatever bullshit train he was about to get on. "In fact, in what world were we *ever* together?"

"How can you say that?" He balks, and I hear Roman snort, amused, behind me.

"Because you were *married* the *entire* time!" I don't care that the person walking their dog across the street turns their head at my raised voice. There's only one person who should be embarrassed here, and it sure as hell isn't me.

He opens and closes his mouth like a damn trout, unable to respond, and I wonder if I'm the first person to call him out on his shit. Realizing he's just a pathetic man with an ego that got too big for his britches has me spelling out the next part slowly.

"Now, you're going to leave my stoop, delete my number, and do me the favor of never having to see your face again, because lord knows you owe me at least that." He opens his mouth to say something, and I wag out my finger. "Uh-uh. Leave. *Now.*"

He blinks, stupefied, before turning around and schlepping down the steps. I stand in the doorway, watching his usually arrogant posture deflate.

Roman wraps his arm across my chest and kisses my temple. "You're fucking amazing."

Lewis drops his car keys while taking them out of his pocket in a failed attempt to get out of here quickly.

"One sec," Roman says before casually jogging down to the sidewalk.

He manages to reach Lewis's keys before him, and when they both stand back up, Roman's at least half a foot taller. And shirtless, his chiseled muscles looking like velvet-draped marble in the sun. While Lewis looks like Captain America before he got the superhero serum.

Roman holds his fist with the keys out but doesn't release them into Lewis's waiting palm right away. Instead, he clasps him by the shoulder and yanks him unwillingly closer. I can't make out his words but can clearly see the effect they have on Lewis, who goes rigid as stone, eyes wide with fear. He nods rapidly, muttering something that looks like *yes, yes.*

Finally, Roman drops the keys into Lewis's near-shaking palm. He claps him on the shoulder. With a friendly but sure tone, loud enough for me to hear, he says, "Alright, good meeting you and glad we understand each other."

I don't give Dr. George Lewis Guzman one more second of my attention. Instead, I look at Roman with a proud smile and watch him take the steps two at a time back to me. In the doorway, he reaches down to hug me, and I jump into his arms, wrapping my legs around his waist and looping my arms around his neck.

I pull him in for a bruising kiss as he walks us inside, slamming the door and leaving one massively mediocre man behind.

SMITTEN MITTENS

Roman

When Cash and Harlow first got together, he sort of, maybe a little, kinda kidnapped her. It was for her own protection after the Bratva had shot up the Den, and technically she was free to leave. There were no chains or locked doors.

There was, however, Alfie and me stationed in the hallway outside his penthouse, armed and ready to stop her by any means necessary, but still not technically kidnapping, right?

I thought he was crazy then—hell, I still think he is fifty percent of the time. After all, sane is never a word I would use to describe Cash Fox. But after Guzman's call and visit, I understand Cash's actions a lot better.[1]

Look, all I'm saying is the good doctor better not show his face anytime soon because I certainly won't hesitate to follow through on the promises I made him this morning.

So when Ren tells me she is meeting up with her old coworker, I'm tempted to whisk her away and throw away the key. Instead, I do the rational thing and give her the brass knuckles from my key ring.

She laughs and takes a sip of her coffee. We're sitting at June Bug's outdoor tables. "We're just going Christmas shopping, then having lunch."

"You never know," I warn jokingly. "People can get awfully desperate when they wait until the last minute to buy gifts, and desperate people do crazy things."

"Don't worry, I'll let everyone know my boyfriend could kick their ass."

My hand in my lap flexes, then balls into a fist as I try to play it cool. "Boyfriend, huh?"

She lifts her hair off the back of her neck and shrugs nonchalantly. "At least for the next forty-eight hours."

---

1. Play "Starving"—Hailee Steinfeld, Grey, Zedd until end of chapter

I trace my back my molars and nod with a smirk before posing, "But I won't be with you."

Her lip quirks. "I'll tell them you go to a different school."

"You got it all figured out." I chuckle. "I've been meaning to ask, what are you doing for Christmas? Going to the ranch?"

She looks away briefly and begins twirling a lock of hair. "Uh, no. I'm just gonna stay in." Her casual tone is forced.

"Stay in?" That's more what people say about New Year's.

"Yeah, my parents were gonna come visit, but then Popeye went missing, and, well . . ." She waves her hand in the air.

"Popeye?"

"One of the barn cats." She partially rolls her eyes.

"Then you'll spend Christmas with me and the Foxes," I say like it's already decided, because it is.

"Oh no, I'm not going to crash your Christmas. Plus, five days will be up." The look she gives me makes me think her last sentence might be more of a question.

Question or not, I know my answer. "Then give me five more."

"Okay." She bites her lip—her tell when she's fighting a smile.

She wraps her hands around her vanilla iced latte as if it's a hot mug that will warm her up. Instead, she shivers a little.

I can't help but laugh. "You know lattes come hot too, right?"

She laughs. "It's not the same."

"We can sit inside," I offer, but she shakes her head.

"I'm not cold, really." She tries to convince me with a long, pointed sip.

I take a pair of gloves from my jacket pocket and insist, "Will you at least wear these?"

"If it will make you feel better," she teases.

"It does," I say as she slides them onto her hands.

And then we just smile at each other like a couple of lovesick fools.

I'm not expecting to see Ren until later this evening, so when she walks into the Den a couple hours later, I feel like a boy in the schoolyard seeing my crush. My stomach swoops and my heart races. Butterflies. Is she here for me?

"So I take it things are going well?" Cash asks with a chuckle, making me realize I stopped talking mid-sentence the moment she walked in.

Ren gives me a small wave and smile as the hostess seats her and her friend somewhere behind me.

Harlow giggles on the other side of him at the bar and teasingly singsongs, "Aww, Roman is in love."

Before I can respond, Cash says, "Don't try denying it, buddy."

The corner of my mouth tilts up. "I wasn't going to."

Harlow squeals and claps her hand, then gasps. "Oh my god, can I officiate the wedding? Cash has done, like, five already."

"Two," Cash corrects dryly. "And be my guest. Maybe Roman will pay better than my stingy-ass, ungrateful, freeloading brothers."

"Oh, big bad boss," Harlow mocks. "Like we haven't all seen the certificate of ordination hanging in your office."

"That's for legal reasons," he tries.

I can't resist chiming in. "Oh, was the three-thousand-dollar Buccellati frame also for legal reasons?"

"Yes," he says stubbornly, then picks up his empty glass before setting it back down, annoyed, looking around for the bartender. "Where's Bri? I need a refill."

"Oh, hi, Ren!" Harlow waves, and I look over my shoulder.

I get up and give her a hug, whispering into her hair, "Hey, baby." She squeezes me a little tighter before letting go.

"Roman didn't tell us you were coming, or we would have gotten a bigger table for all of us," Harlow says.

"That's 'cause he didn't know. I was talking him up so much that my friend insisted on meeting him." She laughs, then adds, a tinged embarrassed, "Especially after she asked if he had any brothers . . ."

"I don't have any brothers," I state, a little confused. I told her as much as a few days ago.

"I know." She grimaces playfully and glances at Cash, who chuckles.

Apparently catching on before me, he finishes for her. "But I have three."

"Ooh." Harlow nods exaggeratedly, then frowns. "Unfortunately, all taken. But probably for the best." She covers her mouth from one side and whispers, "The Fox brothers are kinda crazy."

"Duly noted." She laughs. "I'll let her know she's not missing out."

"Well, I wouldn't say that," Harlow says coyly, giving Cash the same smile Ren gave me while putting on my gloves.

Cash grabs his wife's ass. "Damn straight, *a chuisle*."

She half-heartedly swats his hand away, and I give Ren a *we've been here before* look. She fights a smile and offers, "C'mon, let me introduce you to Eliana."

I'm used to blending into the background. My job is all about the small surrounding details that keep the center of attention safe. So when Ren and her friend spend the next hour unabashedly looking my way, sometimes even as they converse and giggle—presumably about me—it's a new experience . . . one I don't altogether hate.

If you'd asked me before today if I liked being the topic of discussion, I would have given a quick and unequivocal no. I prefer to go unnoticed. But that was before I felt what it was like to be noticed by Serenity Calloway.

Her attention is like a slow-burning flame. The knowledge that I'm on her mind warms me to my soul.

In fact, it's almost all I can focus on. So much so that I suggest Cash and I continue our conversation in his office because I'm only really hearing every other word out of his mouth, too busy wondering what's coming out of hers.

When we're done, I head to the bathroom. It's occupied, so I wait, fighting the urge to peek into the dining room to see if Ren is still here. When the door opens, I'm about to step aside for the person exiting, but then without thinking, I'm pushing them right back in.

"Roman." Ren gasps as I pull her tightly to me, locking the door behind us.

"I'm sorry, sweet girl. I just need a taste." My fingers delve into her hair, and I bring my mouth down on hers.

She moans hungrily, rolling her hips against me as I crush our bodies together. The next thing I know, my hand is in her pants and she's arching her back into me.

"You make me so fucking crazy." I groan hoarsely, dragging my lips up and down her neck.

"Same," she pants. "I want you all the time."

Her back slams into the wall, and she lifts one leg to better grind into my palm, her arousal coating my fingers. "Have you been soaking your panties all lunch?"

"By all the time, I meant all. The. Time—*oh fuck*," she curses, then bites down hard on her lip as I plunge two fingers inside her.

The way her pussy grips them makes my cock strain in my pants. Fuck, I could take her right here. I'm dying to take her right here. So god knows what compels me to slowly withdraw my fingers and gently spread her wetness in soft circles around her clit before withdrawing them fully from her jeans.

She mewls, and I chuckle smugly. "What a needy little thing. Too bad you've signed on for five more days." I clasp her chin with one hand while pulling out my keys with the other. "You're gonna go back out there unsatisfied and desperate for more. I want you dripping in your panties for the rest of the day, and every time you feel how wet you are, you're gonna remember who owns your pleasure. And when you're ready . . ." I press a key for my apartment into her palm. "You're going to come to my place and wait like a good girl for me to give it to you."

Her eyes, which widened when I removed my hand, drop to half-mast. Her tongue slowly glides across her lip. "Yes, sir."

UNWRAP YOU

Ren

After lunch, I head home to wrap the gifts I bought earlier with Eliana. Despite there being quite a few boxes under my tree, only one of them contains an actual present. I wrapped the rest of the empty boxes after learning my parents wouldn't be coming, knowing that if I didn't, Christmas would come and go without anything under the tree.

Thinking of my parents brings the usual jumbled bag of mixed emotions. Especially after Johnathon Willis's arrest. I want to know how it's affecting the community, but most importantly, make sure my parents are okay. Since my mom lost her phone, I've tried reaching her by calling Celeste but have only gotten voicemail. So,

I wrote them a letter and sent it with another prepaid cellphone. You'd think they'd reach out to me given the circumstances, but honestly, the community is so isolated that I wouldn't be surprised if the news hasn't reached them yet. Even if it has, the leaders are all too versed in spinning lies and cover-ups.

Luckily, I get to Roman's present and wrapping it takes my mind off the cynical thought. We agreed to no presents because it's such short notice. But it's just something small. It seemed the least I could do after crashing his family Christmas. If he makes a fuss, I'll call it a five-day anniversary or a "thank you for saving me from spending Christmas alone" present.

I've just finished putting it under the tree when my phone rings. When I don't recognize the number, I wonder if it's mother's intuition calling me right on cue.

"Hello?"

My heart sinks a little when it's an unknown man's voice that answers. "Hi, am I speaking with Ms. Serenity Calloway?"

"May I ask who's calling?" I think for a second it might be Lewis getting someone to call on his behalf, but I keep my tone friendly in case it's the people from the primate sanctuary letting me know if I've been accepted as a volunteer.

"Yes, of course, and apologies for calling on the weekend and so close to the holiday. We are just eager to get the ball rolling as soon as possible. My name is Andrew Doring, I'm an attorney with Hanson and Dwyer, and we are bringing a class action suit against the oil company that unlawfully poisoned your community's water for the past two decades. Now, I don't want to take up too much of your Sunday, so all I need to know now is if you're interested in learning more, and I can email you all the information." Well, I definitely wasn't expecting *that*.

"That does sound interesting, but I don't actually live there anymore, haven't for quite a few years."

"Oh, that doesn't matter. It's your previous exposure that qualifies you. Really, there isn't much you even have to do, as it's a pretty cut and dry situation, unless you've been diagnosed with any serious disease because that could make you eligible for a larger settlement. But even then, we'd just need a letter from your doctor."

I haven't thought about that until now, but it makes sense that it could be a high-risk factor. "I haven't, thank God. But you can send me more info."

I give him my email, and he thanks me for my time, apologizing once more for calling on the weekend before hanging up.

A few minutes later, I receive his email. There's a lot of legalese that I don't fully understand, but it sounds official. I check out the firm's website next. Scrolling through their testimonials page, I recognize a face next to a glowing review. I make a call.

"Hey," Harlow answers with a smile in her voice. "If you're wondering where Roman is, he's still tied up with Cash unfortunately. But you can come hang out with Niamh and me *until Dada gets home,*" she finishes in baby talk, and I hear her daughter's responding happy babbles through the phone.

"Aw, I appreciate the offer, but I was actually calling with a question for Cash."

"Of course, what's up—*oh, no pulling Mama's earrings.*" I laugh. From what I've been told, Niamh seems like a wonderfully chaotic little whirlwind of a baby. I can't wait to meet her at Christmas.

"Well, I was contacted about being part of a class action suit and when checking out the firm's website, I saw Cash is a client of theirs. I was wondering if he'd be willing to tell me a bit more about his experience with them—I mean, I assume it's mostly good if he's given them a testimonial."

"Oh, Hanson and Dwyer? They're great, always trying to take him golfing. I don't know why. Cash *hates* golfing. He turns them down every time. I told him next time he should suggest the bowling alley instead, or the gun range or *something*. But you didn't call to hear about Cash's preferred hobbies."

I smile, laughing internally because she just epitomized everything I've come to learn about the Fox family: members of the criminal underworld to whom the bowling alley and shooting range are equally good options for some good ol' family fun.

"I'll have him call you. Is it cool if I give him your number?" she asks.

"Of course, thank you so much."

Once we hang up, I take the key Roman gave me out of my pocket. Flipping it over in my hands makes butterflies beat in my stomach. Now that gifts are wrapped, there's nothing left to do but *wait like a good girl.*

As usual, Roman's apartment is levels of clean I can only aspire to, except for now his tree is full of color and eclectic ornaments that hold nostalgia made sweeter by the memories of picking them out.[1]

The tree is such a showstopper that I don't notice the sleek black gift box on the counter at first. Out of curiosity, I go check it out and spot a card with *For my sweet girl* . . . written across the front. My stomach flutters as I open it.

> *You know what to do.*
> *I can't wait to take this off you.*
> *-R*

The fluttering in my stomach turns into full-on cartwheels as I lift the magnetic lid. The only time I've received something in a box this nice was when I bought Chanel perfume to celebrate my last promotion. I regretted the purchase instantly. But then, it arrived. Just

---

1. Play "Heaven Written"—Soldana until end of chapter

the experience of unboxing the luxurious packaging was worth the splurge.

I don't consider myself a very materialistic person, but I'm inexplicably touched by whatever this is. That Roman would think me worthy of something so fine after only a few days.

Opening the box, I delicately peel off the embossed sticker sealing the tissue paper to reveal silk and lace in a beautiful, rich red. I gently lift the garment with only my forefingers and thumbs, feeling like I should be wearing the white cotton gloves for handling fine art.

It unfurls into an absolutely gorgeous babydoll negligee. A lace bodice gives way to a sheer, flowy silhouette. Instead of cups, two thick, silk ribbons tie into a large, romantic bow. All of it is the same vibrant, Christmassy red. Festive and beautiful. A man truly after my own heart.

I go into his bedroom to change. I've bought pretty bras and underwear for myself before, but never anything I'd consider actual lingerie, let alone worn something like this for someone else. I feel salacious and spoiled. I straighten the bow over my cleavage in the mirror. I feel . . . *dirty and desired.*

My heart skips a beat when Roman's number lights up my phone on the mattress next to me. "Hi," I say, a smile immediately spreading across my face.

"Hey, sweet girl, I'll be home in five minutes. Can I assume you've done as you were told?" A delicious shiver runs down my spine at the contrast between the husky, adoring way he answered and the stern, dominant tone of his question.

"Yes." I bite my inner lip.

"I'd ask for a photo, but it would be awfully rude to ruin the surprise of a gift."

"But I've already opened it." Shit, shit, that horrible feeling when you realize you've made a mistake spikes in my chest. *Was I not supposed to open it? Did I somehow misconstrue the card?*

"Nah, baby, *you* are my gift."

"But we said no gifts," I tease. My stomach lights up with heat, melting away any fear of having made a mistake.

"It's not Christmas," he points out matter-of-factly, then adds, "There's one more thing I need you to do for me before I get there."

The warmth in my stomach blooms. "Okay."

"Under your pillow, there's something else. Pull it out." I almost miss the fact that he gave me an instruction because *my* pillow. Does that make it *our* bed? I feel like I could jump up and down on the mattress, but instead I force myself to focus and reach under the pillow.

My fingers wrap around something bumpy and metal, and I pull out a pair of black handcuffs encrusted with pale pink gems.

He must know I've found them by the small gasp of my breath. "I'm in the elevator. I want you ready for me when I get there." His words are clipped and dry, but I'd bet my bottom dollar a smirk is tugging on his lips. He hangs up before I can ask any questions.

I look at the cuffs in my hands, confused, my heart racing as I picture him in the elevator getting closer and closer. I glance around for another note, even picking up both pillows to check under them. I can hear the steady ping in my head as it passes each floor.

His headboard is made up of black metal rods. That has to be it. I quickly lock one wrist then loop the other cuff through the headboard before securing it to my other wrist. Seconds later, I hear the front door open.

The sound of Roman's heavy footsteps beats like a drum in my chest. Anticipation and excitement have me squirm in the restraints. My arms above my head make my chest push out a bit, and the light from the lamp catches on the silky bow, making it shine and shimmer with every inhale and exhale.

When he reaches the room, he doesn't say anything. At least not with words.

His eyes though . . . The way they soak me in feels like poetry.

The slight confident lift of his chin and tilt of his head as he slowly undoes every button on his shirt is a king's decree, claiming me.

The soft sound of his clothes hitting the floor, a hunter's whispered intentions. Only I don't feel like his prey. I feel like his prize.

It's only once he's naked that he finally speaks, stepping up to the foot of the bed and asking the same question he did that first night, "Do you have any idea how stunningly beautiful you are?"

This time there is no hesitation or unsure response.

"Yes."

A soft smile turns the corner of his lips and pride brightens his gaze.

"Good." He climbs onto the bed and shoves my legs apart so he can kneel between them. "So, you'll understand why I won't be able to go slow. Having you all tied up and gift wrapped in my bed . . . I can't wait to fucking unwrap you." And with that, he gives a hard tug to the end of each ribbon, collapsing the bow.

Just as ravenous as he promised, he dives down and squeezes one breast firmly with both hands and sucks on my nipple, laving his tongue in circles. I moan and press my chest up into him, but my limited mobility makes me huff in frustration.

He chuckles and looks up at me as he flicks his broad tongue over my rosy peak. "Frustrated, baby?"

"I want to touch you," I protest desperately.

"So you're frustrated that I can touch you all I want while you can't lay one finger on me, not because I made you go all day wet and needy?" As he says this, he starts at my knee and trails one hand up to just barely brush over my pussy. Even with such a light touch, I feel him spread my juices up my slit.

"Both. . . ?" I whimper.

"Is that a question?" He teases my lips apart, making my whole body clench when his fingertips ghost over my clit.

Burning up inside, I push him, "I thought you weren't going to go slow."

I cry out sharply as he shocks me with a fiery slap to my breast still tingling from his mouth. He sits up and lays two more slaps to my inner thighs. They sting like hell, but I still find myself breathless and wanting more.

"Is that how you want it?" There's a teasing quality to his low growl. "Hard and painful?"

"Yes . . . sir?" I said it without thinking at the Den, but it made something hot and carnal twist in my chest then. So, when I try it again, this time for real, it comes out more of a question.

That same pride lights up in his eyes. "You can call me sir. Does it make your pussy wet? Calling me that?"

"Yes," I whisper, and he lightly lifts one brow. "*Sir.*"

"Good girl," he whispers back in a soft but husky purr. "Always so fucking good for me, aren't you?"

I nod, unable to respond verbally. I bite my lip as he slides his stiff cock over my pussy, pressing down on it so it drags heavily across my clit.

With his other hand, he squeezes my breast, then he pinches and tugs on the nipple. I suck in a sharp breath at the quick, biting pain.

"I love having you all to myself like this with nothing you can do about it. The perfect gift," he mutters, then adds, "but you're right. It fucking hurts to go this slow. My favorite kind of torture, but—" I feel his cock nudge against my entrance. "There's only so much . . . a man can *take*." He groans roughly, punching all the way inside me.

"*God, yes.*" The cuffs rattle as I needily press my hips up to take him deeper.

"And you . . ." He wraps the ribbons around his fists, using them like a harness. "You always take me so well."

His words are gruff and come out a little more strained with every stroke. Microexpressions of pleasure twist into one constant face of rapture. It's spellbinding watching him lose himself inside me. We haven't talked much about his work, but I know he carries his responsibilities heavily. But when we're like this, it all just melts away. He sets down the mighty weight.

It makes me want to grab his face and kiss him within an inch of my life. A single kiss can tell someone so much, but without that option, I try mere words.

"Fuck, Roman, you feel so good." *Good?* Why did I pick something so mundane when what he makes me feel is anything but? When what I really mean is safe, cherished, *happy.* "Happy. You make me so fucking happy." It comes out like a plea, as if I'm begging for the right words to convey this mountain of emotion.

Somehow, he must get it, even with me lacking articulation, because his brows crumble together and he sighs deeply. "Me too, sweet girl. You make me so damn happy." He presses his lips to mine then, and my heart thunders with the chance to put everything I couldn't phrase into the tangle of our lips and tongues.

I rock my hips up into him, and he groans against my mouth. "That's it, plant your feet and arch your back, baby. Grind that sweet pussy on me."

My clit rubs against the hard planes of his body, making him tighten his jaw and roughly exhale every time I clench around him.

"Oh god, fuck, fuck, fuck," I stutter, keening. "Please, sir, let me come." My stomach knots with the struggle to hold all the pleasure pulsing just under the surface, my muscles coiling in restraint.

"Of course." He has the same desperate quality in his voice. "Be my good girl and make a mess on my cock. Come nice and hard for me, baby, and I'll fill you up."

CHRISTMAS EVE

Roman

We arrive at Bartlett Farms Christmas Eve evening. The berry farm used to serve as a safe house of sorts for the late Aiden Fox to stash his sons when things got too hot in the city. It hasn't been operational for some time, but the elderly couple who ran it continued living in the main house until their passing. Now, Finn and Effie live in the barn's converted loft apartment and the big house is used for family holidays.

"Flurries!" Ren shouts as we turn into the gravel driveway, pointing out the windshield. And sure enough, my headlights capture the small flutter of light snow falling.

"We're gonna have a white Christmas," she squeals excitedly, despite none of the snow sticking and the radar predicting nothing more than a little ice. A fact I only know because she checked it about every five minutes on the drive here.

"Looks like it," I say, even though I doubt it. Her delight is too sweet to sour.

I crawl down the driveway, partly for my car's sake and partly so I can watch Ren's reaction. "I feel like I'm in a snow globe," she says with awe.

The white farmhouse is lit up with colorful lights strung along the porch's roof. Between the flurries and the honey-like glow from the gas porch lamps, it really does look like a snow globe scene.

Damn, maybe I am a Christmas person after all.

Or maybe I'm just a Ren *person.*

I try to carry all our bags inside, but she insists on helping. My threats to spank her if she doesn't let me have the opposite effect. So, I concede and let her carry the gifts—most of which are for Niamh.

She looked at me suspiciously after seeing them when I picked her up. She didn't believe me.

"Hey, it's not my fault that no siblings mean no nieces or nephews to spoil," I argued, hoping she didn't see her name on one. We said no presents, but there was no way I *wasn't* going to get her something. Especially after my curiosity got the best of me and I shook one of the boxes under her tree.

It was empty.

God, my heart nearly broke picturing this woman, who probably loves Christmas more than anyone I know, wrapping empty presents in anticipation of spending the holiday alone. The thought makes me eager to get inside so I can empty my arms and fill them with her.

I'm so far gone that urges like that don't scare me anymore. Because whether it's five more days or five more years, I'll take them all. I'm done acting like there was ever any other option for me.

We have to add both extra leaves to the dining table to fit us all. There are eight people just counting the Foxes and their wives—well, Stella and Lochlan aren't married *yet*. Then add in a baby, Alfie, Ren, and me and we somehow squeeze twelve people at a ten-person table.

Cash is the last to sit after carving the honey baked ham. He joins just in time for Niamh to attempt a nosedive out of her highchair. Harlow quickly reaches for the tray in his hands as he catches her with one arm.

"Oh shit—*shit*—I mean *shoot,* I knew I was forgetting something," Alfie blunders. "The whole buckling-her-in thing." He waves his hands around, very poorly miming what he *should* have done after putting her in the chair.

"You're good," Cash says, and Harlow, Lochlan, and Stella all look at him like he has two heads. He continues in the same friendly tone while bouncing Niamh on his knee. "But forget again and I'll wrap that seat belt around your neck until your eyes bulge out of your head."

"Ah, there's Daddy Cash." Lochlan chuckles and sits back with a grin. Everyone laughs except for Harlow, whose cheeks turn bright red, and Cash, who nearly spits out his whiskey.

He clears his throat and tells his brother coolly, "Don't call me that again."

"Jesus Christ," Roan scoffs in disgust, and Reggie's eyes widen.

A wave of understanding washes over the table, and Ren who was looking to me for clarity, finally gets it. "*Oooh . . .*"

"Well, this is certainly a holiday for the books." Stella teases Cash, "The one where we all learned you have a daddy kink."

The table erupts in laughter again, and Harlow buries her face in her hands.

"Don't worry, Harlow," Reggie says. "Roan and I once walked in on Finn and Effie in the studio with paint in places it had no business being."

Finn fires back, "That's rich coming from someone who's had a gun in the same place."

"You told him?!" Roan cuts off his brother to gape at Reggie, absolutely scandalized.

"I told *her!*" she defends herself, pointing to Effie, who gives a little finger wave from across the table.

"This is great, us next!" Lochlan cheers.

Stella cuts him a death glare. "You shut your mouth."

Ren looks around the table, possibly more awed than she was with the flurries. Her astonished gaze lands on me and she whispers, "This is the best Christmas *ever.*" She grabs my hand under the table. "Thank you so much for inviting me."

I give her hand a squeeze. "I'm really glad you're here."

Luckily, that's as contentious as it gets until dessert. Effie brings out the tiramisu and gasps loudly after taking off the tinfoil, waking up Niamh, who was asleep in her father's arms.

"Who did that?" Effie demands of the table, appalled, and points accusatorily at a large scoop missing from the corner of the dish.

Everyone immediately turns toward Lochlan. Everyone but Roan. I watch him sneak a questioning look at his wife. *It wasn't me,* she mouths, shaking her head adamantly.

Lochlan denies it, nobody believes him, and with an untrusting glare, Effie serves everyone.

Finn groans at his first bite. "God, this is so good I could marry you a third time," he says, slinging his arm over Effie's shoulder once she sits back down.

Ren leans into me and hisses under her breath, "A *third* time?"

"It's a long story." I chuckle. Before I can explain any further, Niamh starts wailing because Cash won't give her any of his dessert.

"It has caffeine and alcohol in it, baby girl," he says apologetically. "I know that means nothing to you, so you're just gonna have to trust me on this." He tries to reason with her to no avail.

I watch as Cash does his best to distract her while Harlow sneaks him a few bites and wonder if they can go from kidnapping to airplaning spoonfuls of Italian dessert, is it really unbelievable that Ren and I can make it work?

Cash always told himself the family comes first. But then Harlow became part of that family and everything changed. For the better. I've always told myself the job comes first, but what if it didn't?

Ren pulls silly faces, making Niamh giggle and me smile because I'm pretty sure that "what if" is already here.

Ren

When peekaboo and goofy faces are no longer enough to distract Niamh, Roman offers, "Here, lemme take her." Cash passes her off, and she immediately looks three months younger dwarfed in Roman's arms.

"Come on, Mama, have you seen the train?" he asks Niamh while her little hands paw at his beard. He doesn't make any attempt to stop her, even when pets become tugs.

I finish my last few bites then follow the two of them into the living room, which doesn't look like it's changed much since the previous owners. Crocheted doilies are draped over the arms of the plaid couch. Cross-stich pillows and knickknacks, like novelty salt-and-pepper shakers and porcelain angels, dot the room. It's dark but cozy, Christmas lights on the tree and the porch outside giving the space a rainbow glow.[1]

Roman crouches by the tree and sets Niamh down to show her the train tracks around its base. "Give it a sec and . . . choo-choo, here it comes," he says in a hushed but excited tone as the toy train appears from behind the tree.

Niamh squawks and slaps the floor excitedly as it chugs past, the tiramisu long forgotten. I sit on the couch behind them to just watch their interaction. Roman gently redirects her whenever she tries to rip up the tracks or hands her an unbreakable ornament when she reaches for a fragile one.

---

1. Play "wishlist"—Alaina Castillo until end of chapter

He's so good with her, it makes my heart overflow. I can hardly stand it when he fixes the bow clipped to the itty-bitty ponytail on top of her head. Next-level cute aggression, I swear.

I join them on the floor, kneeling behind him just so I can wrap my arms around his shoulders and squeeze him in a tight hug. He kisses my forearm laying across his collarbone, and I could just melt.

"Finn found this in the attic last Christmas, but it didn't work. God knows how long it was up there," Roman tells me, nodding to the train. "After Effie found these cars at a flea market, he was determined to get it running again." He points out two train cars in front of the caboose that don't quite match the others.

"That's so sweet," I say, settling next to him. "We didn't really celebrate Christmas in the traditional sense at the ranch as a community, but every holiday season, we would put up a miniature winter village that spanned something like thirty feet. As a kid, it felt like it took up a hundred tables, but it was probably only three or four. Anyway . . ." I half-sigh, half-laugh, having gotten sidetracked. "It had a train like this that went through the 'mountains' behind the village and came out of a tunnel at the other end."

"That sounds fun. Is that where you got your love of Christmas?"

"No, that was my mother." I smile. "We never celebrated the religious aspect, but every year we'd cut down our own tree and decorate it with as many ornaments as we could fit. Most of them, we made ourselves. Ya know, that's probably what made decorating it so fun, finally getting to see these little projects we worked on throughout the year where they belong."

Niamh crawls into Roman's lap and he picks her up, cradling her in the nook of his arm and reminding me of my favorite ornament. "Like this one year when I saw the cutest ornament in a store. It was a baby chipmunk sleeping under a blanket in a walnut shell. I *begged* my mom for it, but she said no, insisting we could make a better one ourselves."

As Niamh's eyes begin to droop sleepily, he rocks lightly back and forth and lowers his voice. "And did you?"

"Oh, you know it," I say proudly. "The one in the store was all one piece of porcelain painted to look like different elements. We used a peach pit and made the little chipmunk out of clay and felt. I remember I even sewed together these tiny squares of fabric to make a quilt that you could actually use to tuck him in."

"Is it on your tree? I'll have to look for it next time." I nod with a little embarrassed smile and he asks, "Where is it?"

"You have to *really* look for it. I always hang it nestled inside the canopy toward the trunk."

"Why?"

"Because it's cozy and quiet so he can sleep," I admit, knowing full well my reasoning was cute when I was eight but sounds crazy being a grown ass adult.

Roman laughs but not in a way that feels like he's laughing *at* me. It makes me laugh too, quietly so as not to wake the real sleeping baby.

He shakes his head with a loose smile. "God, I lo—" he begins, and my heart stops. "Like you a whole lot, Serenity Calloway," he finishes, still making my stomach somersault. My cheeks flush, and I wonder if he can tell in this light.

"I like you a whole lot, too . . ." I pause as Niamh stretches one arm in her sleep then whisper, "*Mr. Ford.*" Something about addressing him formally and whispered like that makes heat swirl in my core. He drags his teeth over his lip like he feels the same.

I take an exaggerated breath then, fighting a smirk, ask, "So, what were your Christmases like growing up?"

"Well, even though it felt like we went to church ten times in the week of Christmas, it was more about the food than 'the reason for the season.'" He pauses, then chuckles. "Actually, let me rephrase that. It was definitely, one hundred percent all about the food. Except for when it was about the family gossip, either someone having a baby, getting married, or *buried*. So, closer to ninety percent about the food."

"Oh, yeah? What was on the menu?"

"*Menus,*" he corrects, emphasis on the plural. "We'd spend the morning watching Mr. Bingle on TV and fighting over Grandma's biscuits—my dad's mom—then head down the bayou to spend the rest of the day and evening with my mom's side. And I guess there wasn't any specific meal, just a constant cycle of cooking and eating between running around with all the cousins."

He smiles softly as if recalling all the memories and continues, "It was a lot of wild game, gumbo of course, if it wasn't too hot. Oh, and oyster dressing. One year, I'm pretty sure that and dessert was all I ate."

"That sounds amazing. And delicious," I say as Harlow steals her daughter to put her to bed.

"It really was." He sighs with a touch of nostalgia. I know his parents passed in his thirties and most of his family dispersed after Katrina. I'm about to ask him how often he goes back, if at all, when he continues, a fond lilt in his voice. "And music. There was always music, whether we were singing songs as a family or playing Ella and Louis on vinyl."

"They have a record player." I jump up. "What are the chances they have some?"

"I think a better question would be what are the chances it works?" He chuckles and stands as I begin shuffling through their collection of records.

Incredibly, we're in luck. I pull out Ella Fitzgerald's Christmas album, and Roman sets it up on the player.

I feel like a big ol' cinnamon roll again when it starts playing and the others start trickling in from the dining room.

Roman pulls me in to dance, swaying to the swinging beat. He hugs me tight to him with a wide palm on the small of my back, and I beam up at him and say, "Best Christmas ever."

He gazes back, eyes soft and adoring, and repeats, "Best Christmas ever."

I'm still on cloud nine later that night curled up in bed. I pull the heavy quilt up to my neck as Roman finishes getting ready. This old house is drafty and cold outside the main living areas.

I watch as he methodically ties his durag, rolling and tucking the tail, and realize I've never actually seen him put it on. He doesn't always wear one at his place, and whenever he's over at mine, he seems to magically wake up in one.

The care he takes immediately recalls the image of him fixing Niamh's little bow earlier and my heart feels like it doubles in size all over again. I'm sure it's written all over my face because when he slides under the covers next to me, he asks, "What's on your mind, beautiful?"

On our sides, he tugs me closer, his hands spreading over my ass cheeks, and I hook my leg over his hip.

"Seeing you with Niamh makes me want to rethink not having kids," I say, mostly joking. Then right on cue, a sharp wail sounds from down the hall. We both stifle our laughs. "Or not."

He presses me harder against him, and I feel his cock thicken between us. I roll my hips in invitation, and he flips me onto my back and purrs, "But we can practice making one."

CHRISTMAS DAY

Roman

I wake up curled around Ren, who is nestled into a ball with almost her entire head under the covers. It was quite cold last night and is possibly even colder this morning. Though, the temperature did help the full-sized bed not feel so small compared to my king, because we were bundled so close together. Something you won't find me complaining about.

There are radiators downstairs in most rooms, but up here on the second floor, only the bathroom has one. You would think the bedrooms would get heating priority, but I suppose the original owners were the "put on another layer if you're cold" type of people.

The chill gives me hope though that maybe some of Ren's flurries stuck. I can see nothing but blue sky outside the window except . . . is that a light dusting on the muntins?

I get a rush I haven't felt since I was a boy. *Could this really be a white Christmas?*

Do I wake Ren up? But what if it's just a bit of frost?[1]

I strain to get a better look outside without jostling her, then decide fuck it, what's the harm in believing in some Christmas magic?

I slowly rub her thigh until she starts making those sleepy, little noises telling me she's awake. Brushing her hair back, I lightly kiss her neck and shoulders, and her quiet sounds morph into those of enjoyment.

"Ren, baby, look outside," I whisper as she begins to unfurl from her tight ball.

She doesn't have to scoot far to reach the edge of the bed and prop herself up on her elbows to look out the window.

---

1. Play "All I Want For Christmas Is You"—Michael Bublé until end of chapter

The gasp she makes is almost as sweet as the one she made last night when I slowly sunk into her inch by inch. *Almost.*

I sit up, expecting to see a thin blanket of white. Instead, there's a thick, puffy layer of snow coating everything. The tree branches droop, and deer prints look like small tunnels in the otherwise pristine snow.

A cacophony of voices carries up the stairs. Ren looks at me over her shoulder. "Do you think we're the only ones still in bed?"

"Possibly." I shrug. "Normally, Lochlan can sleep 'til noon, but he's like a kid on Christmas. Sometimes I swear he thinks Santa really comes down the chimney."

She rolls over, chuckling but giving me a conflicted look. "I just love being cozy in bed with you."

"We don't have to get up right this second." I pull her into my side, and she nuzzles against me. I run my hand over her smooth hair and unconsciously start twirling a lock. I love the weight of her head on my chest and the way she smells just slightly like my cologne.

Ultimately, it's the scent of bacon that gets us up.

"Alright, Horny Hallmark, it's your time to shine," I tease her at the top of the steps.

We come downstairs to a bustling kitchen and apparently right on time. Cash takes pancakes off the griddle and adds them to the spread of breakfast food already on the counter, while Reggie is pulling tamales out of a steaming pot. She makes dozens every year with her family back home, and we're the lucky beneficiaries of their hard work.

"You were spot on," Ren says with an approving chuckle. "Everyone but Lochlan."

Looking around, I see she's right and, most notably, all the women, including Niamh, are wearing matching flannel pajamas. My stomach drops as I realize all the women except Ren. *Fuck.*

She doesn't seem fazed, continuing on while I stand stock-still, rapidly trying to think of a way to include her. After a few steps, she stops and looks back at me in question, then laughs.

Grabbing my rigid arm, she tugs me forward. "I'm a big girl, Roman. My feelings aren't hurt. I was so last minute anyway, so it probably wasn't even possible to get me a set in time."

"How did you know that's what I was thinking?" I ask, impressed but not really surprised.

"I don't know. I just did—"

"Ren!" Stella calls when she sees us and grabs a gift bag that is by her feet instead of under the tree. "I rush-ordered them as soon as I heard you were joining us. I wasn't sure on sizing, so there's two pairs in there."

Ren holds her hand to her heart. "Oh my god, that is so thoughtful, thank you." She takes the bag from Stella and says excitedly, "I'm going to put them on right now."

"You better," Reggie says, playfully pointing the tongs in her hand like a weapon.

While Ren practically skips to the powder room to change, I turn to Stella. "Thank you, truly."

"Of course. Merry Christmas, Rom." She pats me on the shoulder, then gives me a prying smile. "She's special, isn't she?"

"Yes." My chest fills with warmth. "She is."

Ren comes out and gives us a little spin, showing off the green and red plaid. Everyone cheers, and she takes an exaggerated bow. Yeah, she's special. Most special thing that's ever danced into my life. But so is this family. The Foxes love harder and fiercer than anyone I know.

"*Are you kidding me?*" Lochlan's voice booms over the music and chatter. We all spin toward the sound. He's standing shirtless in the threshold of the kitchen, his long hair pointing in all different directions. His sweats are slung low on his hips, showing a thin sliver of the world's worst tattoo.

"Listen, I held it together when Reggie and Roan showed up in matching sweaters last night because he probably lost a bet or she threatened his life or something, but now this? Matching pajamas *without* me?" He looks at Stella, damn near heartbroken.

"How do you know I bought them?" she asks.

He holds his hand out toward Ren, and I automatically tense. Family or not, if he tries to imply she doesn't deserve them over him . . . "Because you're the only one with their shit together enough to get another set two days before Christmas."

She smiles, sauntering up to him and laying her arms over his shoulders while he pouts. "Aww, Lochy baby, that's so sweet." The kitchen fills with laughter.

His moping lasts all of another two seconds. He kisses her cheek. "You're just lucky you're the most beautiful girl in the whole damn world."

"Would it make you feel better if I told you I hoarded all the crispiest bacon for you?" she asks, lowering her arms.

He slings his over her shoulders and pulls her tight to his side with a lopsided smirk. "Yes, yes, it would."

As we all go back to our breakfast, I overhear Lochlan say, "But seriously, how is it that Roan gets to wear a matching Christmas sweater before me? I mean, c'mon, Roan? *Roan?!*"

Once we have all served ourselves, Cash gets our attention. "Alright, everyone, grab your plates and let's open some presents."

An hour later, the living room floor is littered with torn wrapping paper, but the view of the train tracks is no longer blocked by stacks of presents. Like the dining room, the twelve of us are a tight squeeze in the small room. Ren sits between my legs on the carpet. And Roan and Niamh, the two with the shortest hair, each have about three gift bows stuck to the tops of their heads.

We unwrap gifts one by one. So when Lochlan, who is tucked in the farthest corner by the tree to be able to hand them out, opens up a box, all eyes are on him. He pulls out his very own set of matching pajamas and whoops, ecstatic. He searches for a path out of the crowded room, then looks down at his body in nothing but a pair of sweatpants.

Uh-oh. I cover Ren's eyes and, just as he's pulling his drawstring, say, "Boy, you got another thing coming if you think you're changing into those right here."

His brothers jeer in agreement, and Stella just rolls her eyes with a laugh.

"Alright, alright." Conceding, he sits back down.

Ren giggles as I uncover her eyes and asks him to pass her a smallish, square box from under the tree next. She scoots out from between my legs and spins around to face me, handing it to me.

"I know we said no presents, but it's small, and I wanted to, and you'll just have to get over it, okay?" She tries to give me a threatening look, but it devolves into a giddy smirk.

"Okay," I agree, pulling on the ribbon with, I'm sure, a matching smirk forming on my face.

I carefully slide my finger under the tape so as not to tear the wrapping paper. Once I get down to the box and open it, my gaze immediately jumps to Alfie. "Did you tell her?" I ask him, shocked.

"Huh?" He shakes his head. Ren glances between us, confused.

I nod to Finn to pass me the gift I had him hide for me. He pulls it out from behind him, and I pass it to her. She looks like she's about to say something, so I quickly insist, "Just open it."

My lip quirks as she forces the ribbon off without bothering to untie it and rips the wrapping paper.

She throws the crinkle paper on the floor and pulls out a glass tumbler with lid and straw, turning it around to look at the front design.

"No way." She laughs in disbelief. "But how? They don't sell these in the winter."

I flick my chin toward Alfie. "He's got an in with the owners."

"Pumpkin spice all year round, baby," he says with a proud puff of his chest and wiggle of his eyebrows.

She nods, piecing it together. "So that's why . . ."

"I thought he told you," I finish, holding up the mug she gave me with the very same logo as the design on the tumbler.

June Bug Café.

Where it all started. Where I became a coffee person. Where I learned that some people order iced drinks no matter the weather. Where I left a newspaper, secretly hoping she'd turn it over.

Where I first saw the gorgeous blonde who decided she wanted to be bad, if only for one night.

Epilogue

Roman

Ren's scream rips me from my sleep. I bolt upright, instinctively reaching for the gun in my nightstand, but it's not there. Because we're not home.

"Oh shit, I'm sorry. I didn't mean to scare you." Ren grimaces, sitting next to me in bed, clutching her phone.

My pulse steadies as soon as I realize she's okay. For New Year's, we continued our holiday with the Foxes to Summerland, a private island resort they'd bought earlier in the year.

"No, no, you're good, baby. You're good." My morning voice is croaky, and I rub the sleep from my eyes. "What's up?"

"Oh my god, okay, *so*," she spews, as if biting at the bit for me to ask. "You know how I told you about that lawyer and the class action suit?"

I nod. "Yeah."

"Well, they settled and look, *look—*" She thrusts her phone in my face, bouncing where she sits like she can't possibly contain her excitement. She points to an email. "Do you see all those zeroes?"

"Yes, that's amazing." I actually can't because her finger keeps covering it up as she pokes repeatedly at the screen, but I don't need to.

I already know exactly how much it is.

Because that's the thing about dedicating your life to the job: you make a shit ton of money but don't have anyone to spend it on.

"This is surreal." She shakes her head incredulously.

I knew the moment Ren told me about the gorilla sanctuary that I wanted her to be able to volunteer for as long as she wanted. But from the short time I've known her, I knew she wouldn't just take my money. Then I heard about the oil scandal. It was the perfect cover.

I also didn't want her to feel trapped or obligated. After all, this was supposed to be for five days only. But hopefully by the time this settlement starts running low, my money will be *our* money and she can continue doing whatever makes big and little Ren happy for a very long time.

Ren

Three weeks ago, I thought I was at the peak of my career and about to be engaged to a wildlife veterinarian. I thought all my years of being the good girl were finally about to pay off.

Then it all came crashing down around me. And all I can think is: thank fuck it did.

God bless the soon-to-be divorced Dr. Guzman—I decided to tell Maria, and she filed papers the very next day—because without his deceit, I never would have ended up in the giraffe barn. I never would have awkwardly, though very politely, cockblocked Cash and Harlow. I never would have finally learned the beautiful man from June Bug's name or told him I felt like being bad.[1]

And I definitely wouldn't have ended up here, on the beach of a private island, listening to a New Orleans brass band while waiting for fireworks to ring in the new year.

"Look at those two." He chuckles and nods down the beach. Following with my gaze, I burst out laughing at the scene unfolding a few yards away.

Reggie is currently dancing drunken circles around Roan while teasing the straps of her dress down. "C'mon, Ro, you're allowed to take that stick out of your ass every once in a while."

She's been trying to convince him to go skinny dipping all trip and has apparently decided she is going to do it with or without him.

"Please keep your clothes on." He tries to sound unamused, but there's a hint of a taunt in his voice, like he wants her to push him.

He tries lunging for her, and Effie and Harlow cheer as she sidesteps him and skitters away, laughing. Reggie

---

1. Play "Sexual Healing (Space Captain Remix)"—Hot 8 Brass Band

and Roan square off again as she undoes the zipper down her side, and they continue to egg her on.

Apparently moved by their encouragement, Cash jumps up from the lounge he's sharing with Harlow. He yanks his shirt off before grabbing her hand and pulling her to her feet. He takes off toward the shore, and like pulling monkeys from a barrel, Harlow snags Effie's hand as they run past. The three of them progressively lose more and more clothes the closer they get to the water.

"You guys aren't helping," Roan shouts as they crash into the small waves in nothing but their underwear.

I watch them splash around, a little envious, until I realize there's nothing stopping me from joining them. Something I never would have done three weeks ago, now comes easy. It's freeing realizing that oftentimes, the only thing stopping you from experiencing pleasure is having the courage to chase it.

As soon as I look back at Roman, he's already reaching for Finn's drink. I tug my dress over my head and squeal as I take off after them. Before I run into the ocean, I glance over my shoulder to see Roman taking a big sip of Finn's stolen beer.

I dive under the warm tropical water, invigorated, and pop back up just in time to see Reggie pants Roan. She howls with laughter. He growls something indistinguishable before ripping off his shirt, throwing her over his shoulder, and barreling into the ocean.

I can hardly make out the musicians' countdown over the waves, yells, and laughter. My pulse races as I look around for Roman, somehow having lost track of him. Lochlan has his arms wrapped around Stella next to our row of empty chairs.

"Ten . . . Nine . . ." The deep, velvety voice of the musicians carries over the speakers.

I scream as I'm grabbed from behind and spun around. Roman grins, water dripping down his face. I encircle his waist with my legs.

He pushes my wet hair back to cradle my face between his big hands. "You're everything I never knew I needed."

I rest my forehead on his, overwhelmed and so full of love and gratitude. "You're more than everything I thought I deserved."

"Three . . . Two . . ."

"Make a wish," he purrs right before pulling me to him. Our lips meet at the same time the sound of fireworks blankets the beach. I knit my fingers together behind his head and listen to the explosions above us as I lick the salt water from his lips.

His hands smooth down my back as he pulls back and he asks, "What did you wish for?"

Picking my wish was easy. Whether back home or off the coast of a beautiful, tropical island, his arms are the only place I want to be.

"I bet you can guess." I smile as the water lights up with the fireworks' reflection, like a thousand gemstones glittering around us.

"Well, if it was the same as mine . . ." He holds me closer. "But I was thinking five more *weeks* this time."

"Close." I bite my lip, my heart bursting like the colors in the sky. "Only, I wished for five more months."

He smirks. "Why not make it years?"

Then he kisses me, hot and bright, just like any future with him.

The End.

Dear Reader

If you're reading this, that means I owe you one big thank you! I am so grateful to be able to write full-time and it's all because of you.

As a token of my gratitude, you can read Roman and Ren's frist—now deleted—spice scene. When I originally began writing, Roman and Ren didn't officially meet until the night at the Den. So when he takes her home after the dinner where she proposes her unique way of thanking him, it's their first time together.

While I am very pleased how the story ended up, this original scene is very different. It's slow, sweet, and special in its own right, and I'm excited to share it with you. Oh, and there's crawling. You can check it out at SummerOtoole.com/Unwrapmebonus.

◦If you enjoyed this book, would you do me a huge favor and leave a review? Reviews are one of the best ways to support indie authors. I appreciate every single one and I know other readers do too.

◦If you really enjoyed this book, consider joining my Patreon, where I share NSFW art (including for this book), early access to ARCs, bonus scenes, serial WIPs, and writing updates. Plus signed paperbacks, stickers, and prints of all that spicy art. On the fence? Check it out with a free trial at Patreon.com/summerotoole.

Signed books—including the flip-flop SFW/NSFW cover of this book—and spicy art are also available through my shop at ShopSummerOtoole.com.

◦And if this little foray into June Harbor has made you interested in the rest of the Fox Family, you can check out the tropes and read the first chapters of each book by flipping to the next page.

◦Thank you again for being here.

◦To happily ever afters,

◦Summer

@summerotoole on TikTok and Instagram

Acknowledgements

M an did this book test me—whew!

I wrote it during the hardest season of my life, and not gonna lie, I kind of hated this story for the first half of it. It felt forced, boring, and was far from my best writing.

I was *struggling.*

Which leads me to my first huge, giant, fat ass acknowledgement: to my alpha/beta team and editors.

These women supported me and got me through this period like those crazy strongmen who can push trains and pull tractors and shit.

My alpha team was there for every wall I hit. Every time I felt like throwing in the towel, they helped me rework the story or even just my mindset.

My beta team was full of encouraging (and often hilarious) comments and invaluable feedback. They helped me polish up the story and add more depth to the characters.

And my editors were absolutely incredible, working with my crazy schedule, partially finished manuscripts, and delay after delay so I could get the script to audio on time.

Thanks to all of them, *Unwrap Me* turned into a book that I am so proud of. It's funny as heck, spicy as hell, and exactly what I set out to achieve.

Special thanks to Cynthia R. for backing the top tier of the Fox Family Kickstarter and giving "Dr. Jerkface"—as he was referred to while writing—a name worthy of not one, but two shitty exes.

An additional shoutout goes to Daniel and Calvin for answering all of my random questions, helping me get the details right, and giving Roman Christmas traditions that I wish I could join.

And lastly, I know we're not supposed to judge a book by its cover, but I *hope* you judged this one by its! Ami has knocked it out of the frickin' park and made all my festive, sexy dreams come true.

P.S. If you're reading this from Amazon, did you know that there is an alternate NSFW version of this cover?? I have an author exclusive paperback with a flip-flop cover featuring both SFW and NSFW designs, plus a foil finish and sprayed edges. You can buy signed copies on my shop at Shopsummerotoole.com/collecti ons/unwrap-me

SUMMER O'TOOLE

Dark Desires for Fearless Readers

The Fox Family Crime Syndicate Series

Make Me

Hate Me

Keep Me

Dare Me

Also available in audio